The Marvellous Mongolian

James Aldridge

The Marvellous Mongolian

cover illustration by Carol Lawson
text illustrations by Julie Stiles

A Piccolo Book
Pan Books in association with
Macmillan London

First published 1974 by Macmillan London Limited
This edition published 1976 by Pan Books Ltd,
Cavaye Place, London SW10 9PG
© James Aldridge 1974
ISBN 0 330 24755 7
Printed in Great Britain by
Richard Clay (The Chaucer Press) Ltd,
Bungay, Suffolk

When I asked a Mongolian friend how to say 'Aunt' in Mongolian, the result was a long discussion between him and his wife which more or less proved that you can't simply say 'Aunt' in Mongolian, although there are plenty of aunts there. The point is that Mongolian doesn't fit easily into English. That is why my Mongolian friends may have difficulty recognizing my English version of Mongolian names. I hope they'll forgive me for my adulterations and simply translate my Mongolian 'Aunts', etc., from English back to the original.

J.A.

I

Dear English friend Kitty Jamieson,

I am sending this letter with your grandfather, Professor J. J. Jamieson, because he told me about you and your pony, Peep. Perhaps he will tell you something about me, but in case he does not I report to you that I am a Mongolian boy, and that my name is Baryut Mingha. This letter is being written in English by my Aunt Seroghli who is a teacher of English in one of our Mongolian Institutes for Foreign Languages. I tell her what I want to say in Mongolian, and she writes it out in English (with not too many mistakes, she hopes).

But it is not me I want to tell you about, but the wild stallion that your grandfather is taking home from our distant land to your Wild Life Reserve in Wales where, he says, you keep your own little pony, which will now become the mate and companion of our wild mountain stallion. I hope your pony, Peep, will be a good mate to him. But if your little mare pony is as tame as your grandfather says she is, and follows you around like a dog, then I wonder what will happen when they meet, because our wild mountain stallion is one of the fiercest horses my family (who are horse herders) have ever known.

But I will tell you all about him, and how he was discovered and eventually captured.

We know now that our Mongolian wild mountain horse is the rarest horse in the world. In fact scientists did not believe that any more were left, even in the remote deserts and mountains of our country. In Europe our rare wild horse is called a Przewalski horse, after the Russian traveller who caught one here in 1882. But we in Mongolia call it simply 'tahk', which is why your grandfather has given the name 'tachi' to the captured stallion.

My people once used to hunt the wild horses for their hides

and their meat. But about fifty years ago scientists told us all about their importance, and explained that they were a special kind of prehistoric horse which existed long before man did. They had not changed at all, because man could never tame them or domesticate them. They are exactly the same as the prehistoric horses that you can see painted on the caves in France by prehistoric men. So when we discovered how important and rare they were, our people stopped hunting them. That was more than forty years ago. Unfortunately there were not enough left by then for very many to survive. For the last thirty years most of our scientists, and the scientists of the rest of the world, believed that our wild horse was extinct. They had searched everywhere in our country and failed to find any. The only ones left were a few in zoos, but they were not really wild horses any more.

I had never seen a wild horse myself. Ever since I was old enough to follow our own domestic herds on my own pony (named Beta), I have gone with our herd into the hills and valleys of our district and never even thought of looking for a wild horse, because I knew there were none left. But I had been told by my father and my uncles and grandfather all about the wild herds that used to roam our pastures, where the rolling mountains come down and join the empty plateau, or in the mountain valleys which are too steep for men to go there on a horse.

But one day I was hunting for two of our lost horses, deeper than usual into the empty mountains (where there are many deep little rocky valleys and where nobody ever goes any more), and I saw two strange, dark, reddish horses. You would call them ponies because they were rather small. They were lying down near a new-born foal. I know all our horses, and I knew immediately that these two horses and the foal were not ours. In our country you learn to be very quiet and careful and patient when hunting stray and disobedient horses from the collective, so I dismounted and watched. I could see that they were a different colour, differently marked, and that they had a bigger head – a much bigger head than our horses.

In fact, when I began to think about it, I realized excitedly that I was looking at wild horses – the true wild horses of Mongolia, which everybody in the world thought were extinct.

I just lay there very quietly. I could not believe my eyes. I knew there must be more of them somewhere, and I wanted to wait and see where these two wild horses went. But my own horse, Beta, caught the smell of the wild horses, and he suddenly became very nervous and upset, as if he was afraid of something. My father had told me several times that a wild stallion would fight and kill anything that threatened it – even a man. So I knew why Beta was nervous.

'Quiet,' I whispered angrily to Beta.

I was too late. The two wild horses were suddenly on their feet, trying to persuade the foal to get up too.

'Go away then,' I said to Beta angrily and let him go.

I knew Beta would not go far, and I wanted to stay and watch the wild horses. I still hoped they would not flee. They seemed to be waiting for the new-born foal, but when it finally got up on its weak legs it simply fell down again.

I lay very still. They were now pawing and nosing the foal, and they were lifting their heads nervously in the air. Then one called with his lips (we call it a grass whisper in our district), and I saw a young, furious stallion galloping towards them. He stopped near the horses and the foal, and then stood still, looking up at where I was, on the other side of the deep valley. He stamped his feet, knowing I was there. He was obviously threatening me, even at that distance. Meanwhile the other two horses got the foal safely on its feet and they galloped out of sight.

And that was my first view of the wild young stallion you now know as 'Tachi'.

At first I did not want to tell anyone about the wild horses, not even my father or my sister Miza, or my brother Inja. It is very difficult to explain why I did not want anyone to know, but I was afraid if I told someone, even my sister, scientists would come from all over the world in aeroplanes and helicopters to look at the horses, which would only frighten them and force them to run away. They would probably run off into the neighbouring desert where we would never find them, and where they would simply starve to death. Many years ago just this happened to some wild horses who fled into the desert rather than be captured.

So I did not tell anyone, and perhaps you in England do not think of horses the way we do. The people in our district live from our horses. We breed them and herd them and drink their milk and eat their cheese and use their skins and eat their meat. Some of our houses (tents or yurts we call them) are still made of their hides. This has been the life of our people for many hundreds of years, only now we do it in the collective, and we have our own schools, and our life is more cultured and happier. But nobody else lives with the horse the way we do. That is what my Aunt Seroghli says.

So you will understand that even though we once hunted and killed many of these rare wild horses, it was never for sport. It was only for necessity. As for our own herd of horses – we move them about in the seasons over our grassland pastures, which extend for over a hundred kilometres. So the horse is not just something we ride for pleasure, or work like cowboys in America. It is the main part of all our lives. So I knew I had to look after these wild horses and see that no harm came to them.

The next day I went back to the mountains and left Beta in a little valley and crept up on the ridge above and then looked down at the grassy bottom.

'I am in luck,' I whispered to myself.

The wild herd was back, and this time I could see about twenty-five of them. Some were standing among the rocks, some were lying in the grass. There were four foals, the funniest foals you have ever seen in your life. With their big heads and thick papery legs they looked like those horses that clowns pretend to be in circuses, when they have a man in front and a man behind, with weak legs and a big wobbly head.

I looked for the young stallion, but he did not seem to be there. Then I looked carefully at the hillsides and I saw him higher up the other side of the valley, shaking his head and swishing his tail. That is how I knew him. He was the boldest and angriest of all the young stallions in the herd, that was clear. But he was obviously not yet master of the herd. He was much too young.

My grandfather had told me stories about the way the wild stallions fought each other, and even killed each other, to become master of a herd. Their fiercest fights were over mares. But once a stallion became master of the herd he had to look after it, defend it bravely, keep it together, and keep it moving when there was danger. Above all he had to fight anything that threatened it. I knew that this young stallion would one day become master of this herd, because he was already very clever and courageous. He was the only one who realized now that I was on the other side of the valley watching them, and he ran down and tried to get the other horses to move by pushing them and charging them.

They ignored him, and one of the older stallions finally turned around and kicked him sharply with his two back hoofs, which is the first thing they do when they fight or discipline each other. Tachi (I shall call him that now) turned around and kicked back. But the old one was too quick, and whipped around and bit Tachi on the withers before he could get out of the way. One of the mares with a foal also kicked Tachi, so I knew he was not yet chief, and not very popular.

But Tachi was quite right to want them to move, because I could have been a danger to them. As it happened, their carelessness gave me the chance to go on watching them. And though they were all very nervous, and used their hoofs and teeth on each other all the time, they were not unlike a herd of our own horses, except that they kept chewing the soft hairs from each other's mane and rump, not the way our horses do, but by biting and nibbling and rubbing and butting at the same time. It was very funny to watch, and sometimes I had to hold my stomach and roll over so that I did not laugh out loud.

I watched the wild horses every day that spring, sometimes in the long valley, and sometimes I followed them deeper into the mountains where they spent most of the day lying down, hiding. That meant they did a lot of their feeding at night, which is probably how they had managed to hide themselves for so long. But I noticed that Tachi never lay down. He always kept watching and walking around the herd, sniffing the wind. Once he got four mares together and made them go deeper into the shadow of the hills. But again, one of the old stallions told him to mind his own business by biting him hard on the rump this time.

On another day Tachi got my scent, although I was a long way away, and he tried again to make the herd flee. This time four of the stallions turned on him, and for about five minutes it was a comedy, but a very savage one, because they were all turning their rumps towards Tachi and kicking at him, and he was turning his rump on the circle of others and kicking back. I think they expected Tachi to flee, but though he was kicked very badly (when they kick each other in the stomach that is when they want to kill each other) he did not give in, but dodged them as best he could.

'Don't give in,' I whispered to him. 'You are quite right! I am up here and you should all flee.'

Tachi was always overruled, but it never stopped him trying stubbornly to move the others out of danger.

That is what he was like when I left him in our mountains that spring and went back to school. I still had not told anyone about the herd and I did not intend to. But I was very unhappy to leave him and the herd, because I wanted to see if Tachi would become master. Or rather *how* he would become master.

But school is more important than the pastures, my father always says, so the last time I saw Tachi that spring he was having a terrible fight with one of the older stallions (not the master). They fought with hoofs, teeth and terrible buttings, and I could hear their screams and crashes and grunts, even though I was almost two hundred metres away. He won that fight, because the old stallion eventually ran away when Tachi began to kick him on the shoulder with his front hoofs, which was very unusual. But that was no more than a partial victory, because there would obviously be many more contests to come, and they would probably be much more savage.

But my Aunt Seroghli says that she is now too tired to go on with this letter, so I will have to continue it when she is not so anxious to go and hear our Mongolian singer Norob-Banzad on the radio. She is very popular in our country. Have you heard of her – like Tom Jones and the Beatles?

Incidentally I am sure that Tachi not only knew that I was near the herd, but by the time I left he had come to accept my hidden presence as a friendly one, which is why I felt very close to him. He was the only horse in the herd who was clever enough to know I was there, and at the end of spring, when I went away, he always used to look up in my direction and bare his lips and send me grass whispers of greeting. Or was it a warning to keep my distance?

I do not really know which one it was.

Until later then,

I remain your new friend,
Baryut Mingha

2

Dear English friend Kitty Jamieson,

I will now continue the story of how we caught Tachi, who must be with you by now. And I am sure he must be pining for his wild and untamed life in our mountains, and must feel sad to have been taken so far away from his home.

I left off telling you about him when I had to go back to school, and you can imagine how often I thought about him when I was away, and how I worried about him and the wild herd, which no one knew about. I knew I was keeping the biggest secret in the world. My teacher said that I was day-dreaming all the time, and it was true. I longed to be back in our Altai mountains, and when I was punished for failing to study the history of India my aunt made me apologize to my teacher for lack of interest, and told me it was not fair to the teacher to lose interest in any subject she taught. How would I ever become a cultured man if I ignored the history of India?

Well, summer eventually came, although it seemed like years and years. When I went home to our district in the helicopter, which takes the pastoral agronomists to our collective, my father told me I was not to take our horses near the mountain valleys again, because too many might break away and get lost, or fall into the deep grass traps which were everywhere on the slopes.

'Yes, Father,' I said. 'But can I take Beta in there to look for the white-tailed eagles?'

'Only when the herd is safe, and in the open,' he said.

So I began to follow our herd near the mountains, and then leave them safely in the open country. I would then hurry into the long valley on Beta, going deeper and deeper every day until finally I found the wild herd again. They were all lying on a very steep, grassy slope, and I instantly recognized Tachi among them by his restless walk, and his head-and-tail shaking. He also had a special way of raising his head into the wind like a hunting dog.

Every day for a month I watched Tachi trying to make some of the herd pay attention to him, and every day I watched the older horses attack him, even the mares. Even so, Tachi gradually began to win some of the contests, and by the middle of summer he had become so sure of himself that he was able to keep three or four mares to himself, even though he was still too young to mate with them.

Finally, just before I had my accident (which resulted in the herd's discovery), I saw the old master stallion trying to put Tachi in his place once and for all. The two of them were standing near each other quite peacefully when a young mare came up and lifted her tail in their faces. In a sudden fury the old stallion turned on the mare and bit her flanks. Then he turned on Tachi, and before Tachi knew what had happened the old stallion had a grip on him with his teeth, and with tremendous strength and a sudden twist had tipped Tachi off his feet. That is a very dangerous position for a fighting horse to be in.

'Get up,' I cried.

I was lying near a little cave, and Beta was behind me munching at some grass I had put down for him.

Tachi tried to get up, but the old stallion bit and butted and kicked him every time he tried to rise, and I heard Tachi scream with pain.

'If you do not get up now, he will kill you,' I said.

But the old stallion was standing over Tachi and battering him with his front legs, while Tachi tried to bite the powerful legs as they came down on him.

It was terrible to watch, because the fierce old stallion would not let him get up, and I knew that Tachi would never be able to manage it. If you know horses, friend Kitty, you know how difficult it is for them to get up once they are lying on their side. First, they have to get up on their knees, otherwise they cannot lift their bodies upright. But even when a horse does get up on his knees he is still easy to knock over again, and the old stallion simply waited and kicked Tachi and butted and bit him every time he got to his knees.

It was a hopeless situation, and I knew that I was watching the end of Tachi unless I did something. So I suddenly stood up and ran down the steep slope, shouting at the top of my voice: 'Hoo! Hoo! Hooo!'

At first the two of them took no notice, although the rest of the herd instantly fled in a panic.

Then Tachi saw me. He bared his teeth and whistled a screechy sort of warning, even though he was still down. But it took the old stallion a long time to see or hear me, and I realized then that though he was still very strong and fierce and cunning, he was getting blind and deaf, and was therefore a risk to the herd. If he could not see or hear danger now, they would have to find someone else to look after them, which was obviously why Tachi was trying to take over the responsibility.

Eventually the old stallion saw me as I came running down the slope, shouting and waving my arms. I know now it was a foolish thing to do, because they might have attacked me when I got near, but I was only thinking of Tachi, who managed to get up while the old stallion turned to face me.

I do not know what would have happened if I had not suddenly fallen into a grass trap – which is a deep hole covered by salty grass. I would not have been so careless about these grass traps, if I had not been so worried about Tachi; and I knew the moment I fell into it that it was a bad fall. The next thing I remembered was waking up, lying on my back, looking at our starry black Mongolian night, with all the night sounds of our empty mountains around me – soft rubbing sounds, cracklings, mysterious, silent, funny noises, tweaks, little squeaks, etc. etc. And around me nothing else except the deep hole I was in.

I tried to move, but I felt so weak and had such a headache and a stiff back that I could do nothing but lie there. I knew I must have been unconscious for a long time, and I remembered that poem we are taught at school, by the English writer R. Kipling, which says: 'If you can keep your head when all about you are losing theirs . . .'

I was trying to keep my head, but there was nobody else around to lose theirs, so I wondered where Beta was. I hoped he had gone home so that they would then come out to look for me. Eventually he was sure to go home. But I was so deep in the mountains that I knew it would be difficult for anyone to find me, particularly on this steep slope, and in this deep hole. In fact it was so deep that I knew I would never be able to get out of it by myself.

'And if they do manage to find me,' I told myself, 'they are sure to find the wild herd at the same time.'

That was the bad part of the good part. It made me very unhappy.

But I must leave you there, dear friend, because my aunt says she must begin to wear spectacles. She says it is very tiring to write for long in the light of our oil lamps. We are still out in the summer pastures, and we cannot carry electricity around with us, can we? Though some day we will be able to do it, I am sure of that.

So I will end this letter now so that I can go on and finish the story of Tachi's capture in my next letter.

Until then,

I remain your new friend,
Baryut Mingha

3

Dear Friend Kitty,

I left you in a deep hole, wondering how I could get out of it. And it was really luck that got me out of it.

When dawn came I felt cold and very hungry and wet with dew. I waited all that day, another night, and all the next day, until my elder brother, Inja, found me when he least expected to.

He had been sent to find me (my father and uncles were looking for me somewhere else) and he had been following horse tracks and droppings all day without knowing whose horses they were. At first he thought they were from some of our own herd, which is why he followed them. But long before he reached me (he knew I was somewhere in the mountains) he realized that there must be other horses in the valley. And that could only mean wild horses.

He said he was so excited when he realized it that he almost forgot about me. He had never seen a wild horse either, but he knew as I did that they usually marked their territory by droppings, so he began to look for them. He was making his way slowly and carefully along the other side of the steep slope when he suddenly saw the puffs of dirt that I was able to throw out of my hole from time to time to make little dust clouds.

I will not tell you what an argument I had with my brother about the wild herd. I did not want him to tell anyone. But he is older than I am, and he said we must tell the government so that the herd could be protected. In fact he still had not seen the herd; nobody had but me. But when they took me back to our tents he told everybody the secret, and everybody came to ask me questions. In fact my father was very angry with me because I had kept the secret so long, but I think he too did not want anyone to come and disturb the pastures or the wild herd by looking for them, although he said it was wrong to try to hide them.

When we are in our summer pastures, doctors can only come to us by helicopter if we are ill. When our doctor came he told me I had some concussion, and had pulled all my back muscles out of order, and must be kept on my back for weeks.

It was in those weeks that the scientists began to arrive. I was going to say hundreds of them, but my Aunt Seroghli says that it is uncultured to exaggerate. First came our own professors from Ulan Bator, our capital city. Then some from Moscow, two from Prague in Czechoslovakia, one from Stockholm and one from Hamburg.

Of course they all asked me hundreds of questions. How had I discovered the herd? How had they behaved? Had they seen me? Did they look healthy? How many were there? How many stallions, foals, mares, etc. etc?

I answered all their questions truthfully, but I did not tell them about the young stallion you now call Tachi. I knew that if I mentioned how bold and intelligent he was, they would pay special attention to him.

'Are you going to chase the herd, or try to capture them?' I asked every one of the scientists.

'No,' they all said. 'Of course not. We are here to protect them. They are very valuable. We want to make sure that the whole herd can survive.'

'You will not take them away to zoos?'

'Of course not,' they said. 'We want them to be kept in the wild state. We just want to observe them.'

'They will get into a panic if anybody goes near them,' I pointed out. 'They will run deeper into the mountains, where there is not enough food or water. Or they will try to reach the desert.'

'Do not worry,' they assured me. 'We are not going to frighten them.'

But I do not think they know much about horses in the mountains, wild or domestic. They know a lot of course, they know everything. But they do not know what it is to watch and live with horses. My aunt says I must not be disrespectful. But I only mean that you have to live with horses and follow a herd and know how they think, before you understand how a herd of horses feel or behave.

So when the scientists went out to look for them without me I hoped they would not be able to find them, and they *didn't* find them.

'No luck,' Inja my brother said when they came back after two days hunting for them. 'The old master stallion must be very cunning.'

I did not say anything, but I knew it was Tachi who was being cunning. Some of the professors began to doubt everything we had told them, which made me angry and glad at the same time.

But our Mongolian professors persisted. They used a helicopter to shift four of our horsemen (my father and uncles) to the other end of the mountains, while another group set out from our end. It was not difficult for two groups to converge, and find the herd. Tachi had taken the herd into a very complicated and twisting valley where they could hide by day, while at night they would go out safely onto the slopes and browse and look for the water holes. (Did you know that horses grazing at night in our district consume a lot of water as they eat, because there is so much dew on the grass?)

Of course they found the herd. My brother Inja told me when everybody had returned to our tents that the professors had tried their best not to frighten the herd but only to watch it.

'There was one young stallion,' my brother told me, 'who tried to make the herd run right through us. He must have known it was the only way to escape. But the others would not follow him, and they just kept running back and forth. In fact they got into such a panic that all the professors left the valley so that the herd could calm down.'

'Did the others notice him? I mean the young stallion?' I asked Inja.

'If they know anything about horses they did,' was all Inja said.

In any case the professors knew now how many stallions were in the herd, how many mares and how many foals. They were all very excited when they returned to our tents, and what they decided to do was to leave someone with us who could watch the herd. Or rather keep track of it, with the help of our collective.

'Baryut,' my father said to me, 'when you are able to ride again, it will be your duty to accompany whoever they leave behind, and to show him the best routes into the mountains. You will show him how to watch the herd.'

'Yes, Father,' I said.

The man they left behind was a young Mongolian zoologist named Gritti, who had just graduated at the University of Ulan Bator. But summer was almost over by the time I was able to take him into the mountains to show him how to hide and walk quietly (with a horse and without a horse), and how to avoid the grass traps and how to gallop a horse down the slopes. I told him everything I knew. But he also told me a lot of scientific things about the wild horses that I did not know. In fact I realized he knew more about them, in some ways, than I did. He told me their history, the history of all horses, everywhere, and about the few wild horses left in foreign zoos and how a wild stallion in a zoo will sometimes kill a tame mare if he is put in a small space with her. So I hope your Wild Life Reserve in Wales is not too small, otherwise Tachi might harm your little pony, Peep.

Eventually, Gritti and I were able to watch the wild herd without frightening them. But I did not point out Tachi to him. Often, when he knew we were in the area, Tachi would bite and kick the others to move them on. But only when the old master stallion allowed the herd to listen to the warnings of Tachi's sensitive eyes and ears and nose. Anything else – and the master stallion kept strict control himself, and he was still able to put Tachi in his place with the help of the other stallions.

*

That was how I left them to go back to school again, and I will spare you all the details of what happened while I was away and simply tell you that when I returned to our pastures for what you call in England half-term holidays there were five new professors in our district and they were preparing to capture four horses from the herd: two stallions and two mares.

When I saw my friend Gritti the zoologist I was angry and said to him, 'You told me, you swore to me, that you would not 'take any away.'

'I am afraid we have to, Baryut,' he said sadly.

'Why?' I asked. 'What for?'

'We want to see if we can begin other wild herds,' he said.

'But you told me that you would not send any to zoos,' I said. 'You told me that all the wild horses that were kept in zoos changed their character and became quite different. So why do you want to capture our wild horses and send them to zoos?'

'We are not sending them to zoos,' Gritti explained. He is a very quiet and patient man, a Mongolian who never rode a horse until he came to us. (Fancy that! His father was a miner.) 'We are sending eac horse to a special place where they can copy our wild conditions, a wild life reserve. One of the stallions will go to the Russian reserve on a little island in the Aral Sea (which is really a lake). A mare will go to a wild life reserve in Germany. Another mare will go to Prague. And the last stallion will go to the wild life reserve already prepared for it in Wales, Great Britain.'

'But that means each horse will be alone . . .' I said.

'Only at the beginning. Later on we will give them all wild mates as well. We just want a few of them turned loose in wild conditions first, to see if they can thrive. Then we will try to breed them in the open reserves like true wild horses, not like zoo horses. So you see, Baryut, we are doing our best for them.'

'But this is their home,' I pointed out. 'And horses only like to be where their own country is. That is what our own horses are like; they hate going far away from home. They will all be very unhappy to leave their mountains and they will probably die.'

'Perhaps,' Gritti admitted. 'On the other hand it might also guarantee the true survival of a wild horse, not a zoo horse.'

I knew Gritti and the other professors were doing their best for the wild horses, so I did not argue any more. All I could do was hope that they would not capture Tachi as one of the stallions. In fact I was sure he would be far too clever for them, and I was right. But there was something I did not count on, which was eventually the cause of Tachi's capture.

The way they planned to capture the four wild horses was to box them into one of the long valleys and shoot drugged darts at them. At first my father suggested that our horsemen capture four horses by using the arkan, which is how we capture horses from our own herds. The arkan is a rope loop at the end of a long pole, and a rider simply chases the horse he wants until he can get the loop over its head. We are all taught to do this when we are very young.

But the professors insisted that the drugged dart would be safer and surer and quicker, and would not frighten all the other horses. In any case they would need at least twenty of our horsemen to help box the herd in. Eventually we all set out, with two of my uncles carrying the dart guns, and with four of the professors riding with us. We knew that the herd was now in a little tributary of the longest and widest valley in our mountains. The tributary was open where it joined the valley, but it narrowed down at the other end into a high rock wall. A perfect trap. All we had to do was stop them getting into the open valley, where they could easily escape us.

'You know all the best routes into those mountains,' my father said to me, 'so you can go in with the first lot, Baryut. But you must do as your Uncle Raf tells you. Understood?'

'I understand,' I said.

'Try to help them,' my father said quietly, 'so they do not

23

exhaust the wild herd, or frighten them too badly. I do not think they realize how much damage they can do to a herd if they frighten it, no matter how careful they are.'

'I understand, Father,' I said. But I was really thinking of Tachi rather than the herd.

'They will want the best young stallions and mares,' he said, 'so help them choose the best you can.'

I did not say 'Yes Father,' to that because I knew in my heart I would never help them capture Tachi.

We arrived that night in the long valley, and I thought we would ride out early next morning to surprise the herd. But Gritti said that we would wait until noon.

'That is when they will be most at rest,' Gritti explained to me, 'after being out browsing all night.'

We had to ride in small groups. I was with Gritti and my Uncle Raf who had been given the duty of shooting a drugged dart into two stallions. The other marksman would shoot his darts into two young mares. It was Gritti who would tell my Uncle Raf which young stallion to aim at.

'What happens when the dart hits a horse?' I asked Gritti as we rode into the wide valley leading to the tributary. I was already beginning to worry about Tachi.

'It brings him down in a few seconds.'

'Does it hurt?'

'Not at all.'

'What does it do then?'

'It makes him unconscious for about two hours,' Gritti said. 'So do not worry, Baryut. We are not going to damage the very thing we are trying to protect.'

'All right,' I said. 'But I do not like it.'

We took a long time to reach the tributary because we had to move so carefully. There were ten of us in the first group, and the rest followed, ready to put themselves as a barrier across the entrance to the valley. But Tachi had already heard us or smelled us on the wind, and when we first saw the herd they were already moving up the tributary away from us.

'We will have to ride along the higher slope and keep above them,' my Uncle Raf said.

I knew it was not going to be easy, and though we travelled all that afternoon we did not catch up with the herd until it was almost evening. But this time we had them boxed in the little tributary.

'There is Tachi,' I whispered in the right ear of Beta, my horse.

Tachi was trotting nervously around the herd, keeping it together, waving his head and his tail furiously.

'We will have to get nearer,' Gritti said. 'The range of those dart guns is only about a hundred metres.'

'A hundred metres!' I said. 'We will never get that near to them.'

'We will have to,' Gritti insisted.

The herd was now trotting briskly in a long file (wild horses usually move in single file), with the foals and the mares in the middle, the old stallions charging to one side or the other, and Tachi making a circling movement around the whole herd. They were going deeper and deeper into the little ravine, and it was certain now that we would be able to get close to them when they reached the end of it and were trapped.

'Steady,' my Uncle Raf said and we slowed our horses down to a walk.

My horse, Beta, was very nervous, and I thought then that Tachi had made a terrible mistake, leading the herd into this trap. They were only about 500 metres in front of us; it was only a matter of time. Then suddenly the line of wild horses disappeared around a twist in the ravine.

At first we were not worried because we were sure there was no exit ahead. But when we got to the bend, the herd was nowhere in sight. Furthermore, we discovered that the ravine was not a dead end at all, but suddenly opened up through a narrow gap that we were not able to see until now.

'They have tricked us,' my uncle said.

He was amazed, but I was delighted.

'They cannot be far,' Gritti said.

We began to gallop down the tributary, but by the time we had got through the gap and caught sight of the herd again they were in full flight along a widening stretch leading back to the broad valley.

'Which one of them do you want first,' my uncle shouted to Gritti.

'Any one of the young stallions. Pick any one,' Gritti shouted as we galloped down the valley.

And that was how the chase began. The herd were galloping ahead, with the young stallions in the lead, the mares and foals in the middle and the old stallions behind. But it was Tachi who kept urging them on, biting the stragglers and charging and even pushing the others from behind. But though they were galloping, and though the dust was rising all around us, we were slowly catching up on them, because the foals could not run fast enough.

Then one foal began to lag behind, obviously too weak to go on. The mother dropped back to encourage it, and we could hear her crying out to it. But Tachi would not allow the mother to leave the herd. He ran to her, swivelled around, and kicked her hard to make her run. Then he came back to the foal and began to push it along with his nose. But it stumbled and fell. He refused to abandon it, and he waited impatiently for it to get up. Then he tried to push it up on its feet. But it was too exhausted, and it stumbled and fell again. Then I saw Tachi do something I have never seen a horse do in my life before. He picked the foal up with his teeth and shook it to make it come to life. And he even threw it in front of him. For a little while the weak foal managed to find some spirit, but finally it collapsed again.

By then we were only about 300 metres away and, instead of fleeing, Tachi suddenly turned around and began to run towards us with his head down. He was attacking us so that the others could get away. And it was this very brave and determined behaviour that brought Tachi to his end. My uncle simply stopped dead, waited for Tachi to get near enough, took aim with his dart gun and fired.

We saw Tachi leap and shudder as the dart hit him, but he kept on, and I thought he would reach my uncle's horse and knock him over, or bite him through the neck with his bared teeth. But when he was only 10 or 20 metres away he suddenly fell head-over-heels and lay there.

'We must go on,' Gritti shouted to my uncle because we had all been surprised by Tachi's charge, and the herd was escaping. 'We must get another one!,

They raced on after the herd, but I leapt off Beta and ran up to Tachi and told him to get up.

'Come on!' I said urgently, but keeping my distance. 'Get up.'

He was lying in the dust, panting and snorting. His eye was fierce and he was struggling to get up, working his back legs. He even snapped at me with his teeth, and I knew better than to go near him. But again I told him to get up.

'Hurry up,' I shouted angrily at him. 'You can still get away!'

He tried hard, but his back legs just kept moving helplessly.

I threw a clod of dirt at him to make him angry or frightened.

He lifted his head and tried once, then I saw his neck collapse, his legs stiffen, and finally his eyes closed as he became unconscious.

My aunt says I must now bring this to an end, otherwise you will think that we do nothing in our district but write long, sad letters about our horses. But I did not mean this to be a sad letter. It is really a letter to explain to you what sort of a brave and unusual horse you are going to have in your grasslands, and what sort of a wild and dangerous mate your tame pony Peep will have.

All four horses they captured that day were eventually tied up and taken away from us by helicopter, and a permanent watch put on the rest of the herd. So I lost touch with Tachi. I did not know where he was, or what had happened to him until much later when your grandfather arrived in our district and told me that the young stallion I was so worried about would go back with him to Wales.

Two months had already passed since Tachi's capture. During that time all four wild horses were running free in a large fenced-in reserve near our capital city of Ulan Bator in order to get them over the shock of their capture. But the moment our scientists felt they were ready to be moved, they sent for your grandfather to collect the stallion promised him. He flew first to Ulan Bator, and then came to visit us.

'I thought I had better come to ask you everything you know about him,' your grandfather told me. 'And anything else you know about the habits of the wild horses in their own mountains.'

That was very kind of your grandfather. I knew then that Tachi would be in good hands. So we took your grandfather into the mountains to see the kind of country the wild horses are used to. He asked me thousands of questions, because everybody had told him how I had watched the wild herd for months and months.

I wanted to ask him how he would protect Tachi and about your grasslands and mountains and climate, but my aunt (who was translating for us) said it would be impolite.

But he did tell me about you, Kitty, and about your lovely pony, Peep. And I did manage to ask him one question: 'Is the little mare, Peep, an untamed horse or a tamed one?'

Your grandfather laughed. 'Peep is so tame,' he said, 'that she follows Kitty around like a pet dog.'

That is how I discovered how tame your pony is, and it worries me.

'Peep is a very domesticated little filly,' your grandfather went on. 'So we think she will be able to persuade Tachi to stay in our Reserve until he gets a mate from the wild herd.'

'But Tachi is so wild,' I said, 'that he will never stay anywhere gladly. And he may hurt the little mare.'

But your grandfather laughed at my fears. 'I think Peep's

feminine attractions will persuade him to stay. He will not hurt her.'

I hope not. In any case we all liked your grandfather very much, and we think he is like a friendly, grey, grizzly bear because of his white hair and white prickly beard, and his laughing eyes.

But I will finish now, dear friend, and ask if you can spare the time to write and let me know about yourself, your Welsh grasslands, your little pony, and above all what happens when Tachi arrives. Do you have snow, will Tachi be able to escape, are there many people in your district? You can write in English and my Aunt Seroghli will translate it for me. (She even came into the mountains with us this time.)

So until I hear a word from you, I will end this with friendly and fraternal greetings.

Yours truly,
(Signed)
Baryut Mingha

PS I am sending you one of our winter Mongolian caps with your grandfather, who said you would like it. I hope it fits. Please be careful if you have dogs. Tachi would kill any dog that came near him, so make sure your pet dog is kept out of his way. I am still very worried about your little pony, Peep. Your friend, Baryut

4

Dear Baryut,

I was very pleased to get your marvellously long letters, and found the last one so exciting that I couldn't put it down. Mrs Evans had to take it away from me until I had finished supper. I didn't even feel like eating, I was so excited about Tachi. But Mrs Evans made me eat all my meat, beans and potatoes and pudding and then clear up the dishes before she gave me back the letter and told me to sit down properly and read it calmly. That way I would enjoy it better.

But I'm not a very calm person, I'm afraid. At least that's what Mrs Evans and Grandfather keep telling me, although personally I think I am very calm. But it will take me ages to answer all your questions. The first question I *can* answer is that Tachi is not here yet. He is being kept in government quarantine while they test him to make sure he has no infectious animal diseases.

The one thing I can promise you, Baryut, is that we will make a good home for Tachi here, even though it's far away from his own mountains and valleys. Of course everything here will be a little dull and unexciting for him after your mountains. So when I tell you about our house and our Reserve I'm afraid you won't hear about horse fights and exciting chases through the mountains.

I live on the Reserve with my grandfather and Mrs Evans, who is my grandfather's housekeeper. My mother died four years ago. My father is a geologist, and he has to work in places like Persia or Kuwait (where my mother died); and until he comes back next year I am living with Grandfather who is a Professor of Zoology. He is in charge of the National Ecological Wild Life Reserve, which is a very new, special reserve set up for wild animals that are in danger of extinction, although we haven't actually got many animals yet.

Our Reserve is a large, hilly, grassy area in the Black Mountains, and we have no villages or towns near us, and no real roads except the one that leads to our house. Of course the point of the Reserve is to let the animals live wild and natural, so there are no pens or fences. There is only one electric fence, twenty miles away, to stop animals getting onto a main road. Otherwise we are locked in on all sides by rivers. One of these rivers is on the other side of the mountains, so Tachi will have all the mountains and grasslands to himself, except for some wild goats, stags, badgers, beavers and other small wild animals. That's all we've got at the moment.

Our stone house is in the very middle of the Reserve, and my grandfather's study has big observation windows all around it, with telescopes and cameras everywhere. I go to school in Crickhowell twenty miles away, and every morning my grandfather has to drive me ten miles to the main road, where I catch a bus. When Grandfather isn't here, the postman, Mr Jones, takes me in his van. Sometimes, when we are snowed in, I can't get to school at all. But it isn't as wild as your mountains, Baryut, even though people here think it is very remote. They keep saying to me, 'Don't you find it lonely out there, Kitty? All by yourself?'

But I love it, and I never, never want to leave it.

My grandfather and Mrs Evans are very kind, and I think they both spoil me, although they both think they are being very strict with me. They are always quarrelling, I'm afraid. But it's not bad quarrelling, it's just the way they've learned to get on.

'That woman'll be the death of me,' my grandfather always growls when Mrs Evans accuses him of something.

'He's got no sense of right or wrong, that man,' Mrs Evans says when my grandfather accuses her.

Then they start saying 'Nonsense' to each other because

that's their favourite word when they start arguing. But I love them both.

In fact I feel I have to look after them. My grandfather is very untidy, and when he has finished with a book or map or file or photograph he simply drops it where he is – on the floor, chair, table, staircase. I have to keep picking everything up after him and putting his study in order, although he growls at me when he sees me doing it.

As for Mrs Evans, she can't see very well. In fact she can hardly see at all. She only sees a small area just in front of her through her thick glasses, so I have to make sure that chairs and tables (and my grandfather's books) are not left in the way to trip her or hurt her. I have to be sure that everything in the kitchen is where she can see it – knives, plates, pots, knitting. If something is out of place, she would never be able to find it. I think she must have a sort of film in front of her eyes, because she always carries a duster and she always seems to be clearing the air in front of her, as if she's wiping a dirty window.

So you see I am very lucky. In fact I only mention all this so that you will know what sort of a home Tachi is coming to.

Of course the real problem is my darling pony, Peep, and whether she will get on with Tachi. I would love to say that I'm not worried about her, but that would be a lie. I'm very worried. Peep is so gentle and tame and so trusting that I can't imagine what she'll do when she's put together with a fierce stallion as wild as Tachi is. I can't imagine it at all.

When Grandfather first brought Peep home over a year ago he told me she would some day become the mate for a fierce and wild Asiatic horse he hoped to get from Mongolia. But Peep was already so gentle and docile, even when she first arrived, that I asked my grandfather why he wanted such a gentle little pony to become the mate of a wild horse.

'Because we'll have to persuade the wild horse that we are not enemies. That he can trust us. That far from threatening

him we will help him. You cannot reason with a horse, can you? So what better way of adapting him to our mountains than to give him a clever and friendly young mate who is willing to trust us, who will walk close to us of her own free will, and who will not get into a panic if we appear on a hillside near them when they are together.'

'How do you know they'll find a wild horse in Mongolia, if they're supposed to be extinct?' I asked him. (This was a whole year ago.)

'Because I'm convinced they'll find a wild horse sooner or later, and my friends in the Academy of Sciences in Mongolia have promised me one if they find a herd with more than twenty horses in it.'

'But what happens afterwards?' I asked him. 'Will Peep stay with the wild horse forever?'

'No. Just until he's learned to trust us. Then we'll bring him a wild mate from Mongolia and you can have Peep back again for yourself.'

'But she's so tame!' I kept saying to him.

'The tamer she is, the more useful she'll be,' Grandfather said. 'So you can do anything you like to keep her close to us, Kitty, except bring her into the house, or ride her.'

And that was how we got Peep a year ago. Her real name is Petite, which means 'little' in French. I suppose it is silly to give a French name to a Shetland pony, but she really *is* petite. She is so little and pretty and neat that her name just came out in English as 'Peep'.

At first I used to leave Peep behind when I went walking over the mountainside with my dog Skip. Skip is a Skye terrier, and he never walks, not even in the house. He skips and bounces like a ball, from one place to the other. But one day Peep began to follow us, so I began to tease her, trying to lose her. And she enjoyed the game so much that it became a habit. Now Peep and I do it all the time, even outside around the house. We are always playing tricks on each other. And because she hates to be left out of anything, she is always trying to get inside the house. She does everything to get in, and she becomes furious and whinnies angrily every time I close the door in her face.

I'm terrified in fact that if she does manage to get in one day, Mrs Evans won't be able to see her in time, and there will be a terrible situation. Or, if Peep ever gets into my grandfather's study she'll probably eat up all his maps and letters and papers. She loves eating paper. So it's always a big business keeping her out of the house, although personally I think she would just lie down in front of the fire like a dog, or curl up on the mat like a cat.

Yesterday Mrs Evans came into my grandfather's study with some net curtains and said: 'Look what that pony's done to these curtains! She's eaten the bottom clean off them.'

My grandfather grunted and glanced at the curtains without any real interest in them. 'I suppose she was trying to get in through the window,' he said. 'So what do you expect?'

'Nothing of the sort,' Mrs Evans said. 'That pony does things like that to annoy me. That pony knows I won't let her in the house, so she does everything she can to pay me back. The other day when she got half way into the kitchen and I pushed her out, she picked up the mat in her teeth and ran off with it down to the river.'

Grandfather just laughed. 'She likes your company, that's all it is.'

'Mischief, more likely,' Mrs Evans said. 'You spoil that girl, and she spoils that pony.'

'You're the one who spoils them,' my grandfather replied angrily.

And then they began saying 'Nonsense' to each other, as usual.

Even if I'm not there I always know everything they say to each other when they quarrel, because Mrs Evans always tells me what she said to Grandfather, and Grandfather always tells me what he has said to Mrs Evans.

But I seem to be just rambling on when in fact I should bring this to an end. Both Mrs Evans and Grandfather keep telling me that I'm always rambling, but I had to tell you about Peep and our Reserve so that you won't worry too much about Tachi. I only hope your Aunt Seroghli will be able to understand my handwriting, and will also have time to translate everything for you.

So now I'm waiting excitedly for the first sight of Tachi, and even though I'm very worried about what he'll do to Peep, I can't wait to see what actually does happen when they meet. Grandfather says that I have to keep telling myself that they are horses, not human beings. He means that I must not get sentimental or silly about them. I try not to, but it's rather hard when you are as fond of Peep as I am.

So goodbye for now, and I promise to write to you the moment Tachi arrives.

Your new friend,
Kitty Jamieson

PS The Mongolian cap was fabulous. Nobody here has ever seen anything like it, and I'm dying for the winter to come so that I can wear it to school. I'll have to think of something special to send you in return, but I can't think of anything that will be half so good. Kitty

5

Dear Baryut,

Tachi is here!

He arrived on Friday in a horse box from the government quarantine station in Berkshire, and when the Land
Rover pulled up with the horse box behind it, the vet with it
asked Grandfather if he wanted Tachi released somewhere
in the fields near the house, or somewhere out on the
mountainside.

Grandfather said, 'Turn him loose here. Let his first
view of the place be a view with us in it.'

I didn't know what to expect, and though Peep was
standing behind me, nudging me, and Skip had been locked
up in the house so he wouldn't bark, I felt something quite
extraordinary even before I saw Tachi. I suppose it was
excitement, but I think Peep also knew that whatever was in
that horse box was something to do with her, and that it
was also something mysterious and wild. She kept trying to
put her head under my arm, and she kept nudging me in the
back as if she wanted me to go away and take her with me.

'Shush, Peep,' I told her angrily in a whisper.

I didn't even know why I whispered, but I could hear
Tachi breathing angrily in the box, as if he sensed trouble
outside. He was snorting and stamping his feet and kicking.

'Stand back, Kitty,' Grandfather said, and he told the
vet to open the tailgate.

The moment the vet undid the latch of the tailgate Peep
started to back away. Then she turned and ran away to the
other side of the house.

Grandfather laughed and said, 'She'll change her mind.'

Then the gate came down, and as Tachi backed out inch
by inch I knew I was looking at a completely new and very

wild-looking animal, of a kind I'd never seen before. I'd never seen a horse like him, and I pulled a face and said, 'But he's ugly!'

I didn't expect to see a horse that was so square and so powerful and so shaggy and so patchy, with half his fur (because it doesn't look like hair) coming out. And his extraordinary mane that stands up straight like a toothbrush. But most of all his enormous head. He actually does look just like those prehistoric horses my grandfather has on his charts up on the walls. And whiskers! I've never ever seen a horse with what my grandfather calls 'mutton chop' whiskers before.

'Isn't he a beauty?' my grandfather said as he came out.

'He's awful,' I said, although I didn't mean to say it. 'He looks mad!' In fact I was terrified of him.

My grandfather just laughed. 'You'll change your mind,' he said.

And I think Tachi had already begun to change my mind as he stood there for a moment – just a moment – looking at us with his head down as if he was getting ready to charge. And because he looked so fierce and frightening, I remembered all the things you had said about him when you were chasing him, how courageous and stubborn and undefeated he was. So I didn't really mind how ugly he was.

But I said to my grandfather, 'He'll never be happy here, Grandfather. He's much too wild and different. He'll *never* settle down!'

'We'll see,' my grandfather said as Tachi suddenly hunched up his shoulders like a huge cat, as if he was going to attack. But he suddenly galloped across the grasslands as fast as he could go. He kept galloping as if he was trying to flatten himself on the ground with his odd-looking, thick little legs. He completely disappeared into the valleys. And even then I think he kept galloping on and on.

'Marvellous!' my grandfather said happily. 'Wonderful! What a horse! Superb!'

I looked around for Peep, but she was now hiding in terror behind the house. Grandfather hit his knees and laughed happily into his prickly whiskers.

'Now we'll wait for Peter to report,' he said. 'I'll contact him in the Crow's Nest and tell him to keep his eyes open from now on.'

The Crow's Nest is a glass-sided observation post we have on the highest mountain in the Reserve, and it is so difficult to get to that Grandfather won't let me try to climb up there. Peter is Grandfather's assistant, and he has to stay up there summer and winter watching all the animals. He can see for miles and miles all around. Next year they are going to put closed-circuit TV cameras in the Crow's Nest so that we will be able to see everything that's going on from Grandfather's study. Grandfather is too old to get up there now, except by helicopter. So now we went back into the house to radio Peter with the special transmitter we have in the study, and as I passed Peep she ran away from us, for the first time, as if she knew that we had done something wrong to her.

'It's working already,' my grandfather said.

'What's working?'

'Trouble, at the moment. But Peep's already aware of what's happening. She knows . . .'

I didn't ask him what it was that Peep knew, but anyway that was the beginning of it.

But as far as I could judge I knew that the two of them would never get together. Peep would never leave the fields around the house. And Tachi would never come near the house. In fact I was sure that Tachi was already looking for a way to escape.

But Grandfather said, 'Patience, sweetheart,' and told Peter on the radio to report to us the moment he saw Tachi.

'What do you expect the wild horse to do?' Peter asked Grandfather over the loudspeaker.

'I don't honestly know,' Grandfather said. 'But he can't

do much except find an isolated spot and call it his own for the time being.'

Which is what he eventually did. Peter called us excitedly from the Crow's Nest the next morning when we were eating breakfast. (Peter is a small man who loves to dance, and because he is so alone up there he dances all the time. I mean Scottish and pop dances and even Russian and Hungarian dances – all by himself.)

'I can see the wild horse now, Professor,' he said. 'He's hurtling around all over the place, looking desperately for a way out, or he's hunting everywhere for the rest of his herd.'

'Excellent!' Grandfather said. 'Try to keep him in sight.'

And every day after that, at all sorts of hours, Peter would report what Tachi was doing. Peter was always excited. In fact there is something extraordinary about Tachi that always makes you feel excited, as if you know that he's going to do something unusual, or something terribly wild. I feel it all the time. And Grandfather feels it.

'Even so,' I said to Grandfather, 'he must be terribly lonely and unhappy over there.'

'That's true,' Grandfather said. 'He's a herd animal, so he'll miss the rest of the herd. But we'll let him get a little lonelier before sending Peep over to him.'

I didn't say anything, because I knew that Peep would never go near him, let alone stay with him.

Peter kept watch on Tachi for a whole week, and after he had exhausted himself galloping furiously all over the Reserve (sometimes completely disappearing) he decided one day to stay in a little valley which had some sort of salty grass in it and a sandy bottom, as well as water.

'He's so marvellous to watch,' Peter told us on the radio. 'He waves his head and tail furiously all the time, and looks up at the hills all around as if he's searching for something. He chases everything in sight, particularly horses, sheep and birds. The other day I saw him set out into the mountains after one of the mountain goats. He even had a go at some of the rooks, who flew off as if they were being chased by the devil. Marvellous horse, Professor! Marvellous! He picked the one valley where you would have a difficult time catching him.'

'All right,' Grandfather said one morning after Peter's usual, enthusiastic report. 'We'll take Peep over to him this afternoon.' Then Grandfather laughed in his usual teasing way and slapped his knees, and said, 'I'd give my right arm to see what happens when they finally come nose-to-nose. I suppose Peep will snub him.'

'Maybe Tachi will hurt her.'

'Not in open country,' Grandfather said. 'That only happens in zoos.'

'And you're just going to turn Peep loose out there and leave her?'

'Yes. The time for it has come, sweetheart,' Grandfather said with a sigh.

'It's cruel!' I said.

But Grandfather became very serious. 'No it isn't,' he said. 'Animals are not people, Kitty. I'll go on repeating that until you understand it. In the long run Peep will be better off behaving like a horse rather than a pet. You'll see.'

But I was terribly unhappy when we put Peep in our old horse-box and set off in the Land Rover towards the Tirion valley, where Tachi was. And Peep was very unhappy. She didn't like what was happening. She avoided being caught, and being put into the horse box. And when we started out she let out a terribly angry cry. Even Mrs Evans, who is always complaining about Peep, stood at the door shaking her head as if we were doing something terrible.

Grandfather had looked at the maps and decided that if he left Peep beyond the valley where Tachi was, and in a certain position, Peep would have to pass through Tachi's, new territory as she found her way back home.

'She'll probably reach Tachi's part of the country just after dark,' Grandfather said. 'So Tachi will not be nervous about coming out to take a look at this visitor in darkness.'

'Peep will die of fright!' I said, almost in tears as we reached the little copse where we would leave Peep.

'Nonsense,' Grandfather said. 'Peep will be as curious as Tachi is. Believe me.'

'But he's a wild beast,' I protested.

'I don't think that will worry Peep very much,' Grandfather said with a chuckle, which made me so furious that he pulled my hair a little and said, 'Now calm down.'

'He'll kill her!' I blurted out, and I couldn't hold back my awful sobs now because we had taken Peep out of the box, and she stood there looking at us as if we were monsters. I felt like a monster who was doing something mean to her. And when we drove off, Peep galloped after us until we were going too fast for her to follow. Then she stopped and just stood there, looking forlornly after us as we disappeared.

'She'll get lost . . .' I said, trying not to weep all over the place.

'Oh, nonsense!' Grandfather said, trying to cheer me up. 'A horse can find its way home better than a dog. You could put Peep down as far north as Scotland, and she'd find her way home.'

But I didn't care what Grandfather said, and though I knew I was being hysterical and a bit silly, I kept putting myself in Peep's place and wondering how *I* would feel if I were sent off to face a wild Asiatic stallion alone in the mountains.

That's all I can manage today, Baryut. I'm so exhausted. I've been writing this sitting up in bed. It's after midnight. But I can't sleep. I keep thinking of Peep trying to find her way home through those mountains. There is also a terrific storm going on, lightning that lights up all the hills and grasslands; and thunder and torrents of rain. The thunder sounds like the whole earth cracking open. So I'll finish this now, because I want to bury my head under the blankets so that I can't see the lightning and can't hear that awful banging.

* * * * *

Some days later!

After we left Peep in the mountains I honestly didn't expect to see her alive again. But the next night at about 2 a.m. I was awakened by a noise at the window. It was Peep trying to get her face inside. She was whinnying and making a terrible racket, and Skip was growling under the bed wondering what it was.

'Peep,' I said and leapt out of bed. 'You're back.'

Peep looked at me as if to say, 'Of course I'm back! And what made you leave me out there in the first place?'

I crawled out of the window and gave her a hug and looked at her closely in the light from the window to see if she was wounded anywhere. Then I took her to her shelter in my bare feet, saying 'Shhh!' to Skip as he kept snapping at Peep's heels. When I settled her in the little shed I crawled back through the window and slept happily until it was time to go to school next morning.

Of course Grandfather said, 'I told you so.'

But I noticed that he also inspected Peep very carefully to see if she had been injured, and he gave her a piece of sugar, which he would never let me give her. But she was all right, so I went off to school (back to school ages ago) feeling much better. But when I came home that night Peep was gone again.

'Back to the valley,' Grandfather said.

I was upset again, and failed to do my geography home-work, for which I was punished. And the next night when Peep was not back, Mrs Evans brought me in a cup of hot cocoa and whispered, 'You can keep Skip in the bedroom with you tonight if you like.'

Skip is under my bed every night but Mrs Evans never sees him, so I whispered back, 'Thanks very much, Mrs E.,' and gave her a kiss and felt a bit better.

This time Peep came back after two nights and two days. She looked awful. She was covered in mud, and this time my grandfather pointed to a little patch on her flank as if something had bitten away some of her hair.

'Tachi's attacked her!' I said. 'It's a bite.'

'Nonsense,' Grandfather said, 'It's just a friendly nibble.' And he called Peter on the radio. 'Next time, Peter,' he said, 'you might get a glimpse of them both together. So keep your glasses on the valley.'

'Okay, Professor,' Peter said.

'You'll wear her out if you keep sending her back,' I protested when Grandfather said he would take her back once more.

'She can always lie down and rest,' he said. 'Then maybe Tachi will seize the chance to get acquainted with her.' Grandfather was being very annoying in his teasing way. He forbade me to be sentimental about Peep.

To cut a long story short, we took Peep to the other side of the valley five times in five weeks, and five times she came back. But the last two times she stayed away four days, and she began to be quite different. She still followed me about on Saturdays and Sundays, when we let her rest a bit, but she no longer tried to get inside the house, and once she actually wandered away from the house, as if she was thinking of going back to the mountains of her own accord.

'It's working,' Grandfather said gleefully as we watched her through his glass window.

'She'll never leave us!' I argued angrily.

'She might not go too far away from us when she is here, near the house,' Grandfather admitted. 'But next time she walks through that valley, who knows?'

On the Monday, when he took her off again, I no longer felt worried for her safety, but I was beginning to feel miserable, because I knew I was losing Peep. I knew it.

This time, in fact, she didn't come back. Four days passed, five days, a week, and then one morning at 7 o'clock Peter's voice cracked excitedly on the radio, shouting that he could see the two of them clearly in the valley.

'The wild horse is just leading her around, and she's following him at a respectful distance. He looks like a little king showing his bride her new domain.'

'Excellent!' Grandfather said in his grizzly way. 'Keep a note of everything they do, Peter, particularly their direction if you can follow it.'

'I'm pretty sure that Tachi is already looking around to see how far he can go,' Peter said. 'Can he get across the river?'

'No. They're notoriously afraid of water,' Grandfather said.

'Well, I think he's trying to find a way out. He's all over the place.'

'Naturally,' Grandfather said. 'But I think Peep'll change his mind for him.'

And that was really what we were waiting to see now: whether Peep could persuade Tachi to settle down. After all, that was what Peep was supposed to do.

I had a bit of a secret weep that night, as I thought of the old Peep I knew, and the new Peep who was obediently trailing behind a wild stallion in the mountains. I didn't want to feel badly, but I just couldn't help it, and I kept telling myself that Peep would never be the same again. Skip jumped up on the bed and licked my face a couple of times (he loves salt, and tears are very salty), but I just went on weeping until Grandfather came in and pulled my hair and said gruffly, 'Now that's enough! It's not you out there, sweetheart. It's a Shetland pony, a moor pony, and she's supposed to be out there.'

But I kept feeling as if I was out there with her, and I hated that. If I hadn't been so tired I would probably have started weeping all over again. But Mrs Evans came in and started to accuse my grandfather of being cruel to that pony. To which Grandfather said, 'Nonsense!' And off they went. They were still arguing out in the kitchen when I went to sleep with Skip curled up on my feet.

So we all waited.

At first Peep stayed away from the house, and Peter reported that the two of them were making tremendous and determined excursions into the mountains and through the valley. They were always in a hurry, so that Peep had to canter from time to time to keep up. Sometimes Peter didn't see them for days on end, but they would always come back to Tachi's 'headquarters' in the Tirion valley. Then Peter began to warn Grandfather again that Tachi was bent on escaping.

'I've got the wavelength of that wild horse,' Peter said, 'and nothing's going to stop him, Professor, not even Peep. He's going to get out.'

'We'll see,' was all Grandfather said.

A whole week passed and Peter didn't see them, and even my grandfather was beginning to be worried. Sometimes I would go up on the little mountain near the house and look all around the valleys for them. But they had just disappeared.

Then one night, at about 2 a.m., Skip began to bark under my bed, as if he was afraid of something. I woke up and told him to be quiet. But I thought I saw something outside. I got up to look out, and it was Peep. And though I said, 'Shhh,' to Skip, 'it's Peep come back,' Skip kept barking, and I had to crawl out of the window to see what was wrong.

Peep was muddy and untidy and very restless, and she wouldn't let me touch her at first. Then Skip ran off into the darkness barking at something, which woke Grandfather. He came outside with a torch asking me what on earth I was doing in the cold in my dressing-gown and with no shoes on.

'It's Peep . . .' I said.

Grandfather said 'So it is. I wonder what brought her back.'

'She got lonely,' I said confidently.

'Nonsense, Kitty,' Grandfather said, and he tried to catch Peep, but she backed away. 'You catch her,' he told me. 'She's nervous about something.'

'She's different too,' I said. I approached Peep very carefully, and though she allowed me to get a grip on her mane, she tried to pull away.

'Peep,' I said indignantly. 'What's the matter?'

I pulled her over to Grandfather and he shone the torch on her. She looked half wild. She wasn't so neat anymore, she was rougher and harder looking, and covered in mud and burrs.

'Something's up,' Grandfather said as he inspected her. 'Look.' He held the torch on her chest, just under her neck.

There was a deep mark, a shallow cut, right across her chest in a thin straight line.

'Tachi's attacked her again,' I shouted angrily.

'No. No. It's a wire mark,' Grandfather told me. 'She must have run into the fence.'

'You mean the electric fence?'

'Of course.'

'It must have burned her!

'Nonsense,' Grandfather said impatiently. 'It would only give her a bit of a shock. But she must have galloped right into it to make that mark.'

'It's Tachi's influence,' I said furiously.

Skip was still barking out in the darkness. 'Tachi's obviously out there somewhere,' Grandfather said. 'And not far away. In fact you'd better call off Skip, because if Tachi gets near him . . . Well . . . Just get him in.'

I ran after Skip, who was crouched in the dark with his little ears back, looking brave and afraid at the same time, and barking at something unseen. I picked him up and told him to be quiet, but he kept growling.

'And you'd better go inside too,' Grandfather told me. 'We don't know what the wild horse might do. Obviously he doesn't like Peep being here. So you'd better get inside.'

'What about Peep?'

'I'll wash the cut and then leave her.'

I was climbing back through the window when Grandfather saw me. 'Good heavens,' he said. 'What are you doing! Get down this minute and go in through the kitchen door.'

So I went through the kitchen door, but as I did so Peep came after me and nuzzled me a little, and I knew then that she had suffered some sort of shock and wanted comforting. But the moment I put my arm around her neck she shook me off and pulled away.

'She doesn't seem to know what she wants,' I said sulkily.

'She obviously wants a bit of you and a bit of Tachi,' Grandfather said. 'So maybe everything's working out just fine. We're winning.'

But in a way, Baryut, I knew that I was losing. Grandfather washed the cut, and then we turned out all the lights and watched Peep through my window. She stayed a little while, came right up to the window once, and then as if making up her mind she turned and ran off.

I suppose that was the last time Peep came close to the house, although I honestly think that she tried to get Tachi closer to us. One morning Grandfather called excitedly from his study just as we were about to leave for school:

'Kitty. Look.'

I rushed to the big window of his study and he pointed across the valley to the mountains near the house. Tachi and Peep were walking up the side of the steep slope. They stopped near a large rock, and Tachi waved his head about angrily, exactly the way you described, and he seemed to be sniffing the air in our direction.

Then Peep suddenly turned around as if she was heading back to the house.

'Now we'll see,' Grandfather said.

What we saw was Tachi turning and going after Peep. When he reached her he simply pushed her sharply with his nose. She hesitated a moment, but then she turned around and followed him again.

'He bit her,' I said.

'No, he didn't,' Grandfather said. 'He just nibbled.'

'She wanted to come down!' I said.

'Of course. And some day she'll bring him closer. She's already got him into our valley. So he's obviously settling down.'

But I didn't really believe it, Baryut, and neither does Peter who reports from the Crow's Nest that Tachi is limping, as if he too had a brush with something like the fence.

'I think he's trying to kick the fence down,' Peter said. 'And he'll do it, too.'

'Don't be ridiculous.' Grandfather said.

Nonetheless he sent out Mr Selby (one of the rangers who lives in the cottage by the road) to check the entire fence. So I end this letter, Baryut, hoping that this doesn't leave you as unsettled and confused as it does me, because I don't honestly know whether Peep is winning or Tachi is.

In any case we all seem to be waiting, as if we all know that Tachi will try to do something extraordinary. Something is bound to happen. We can feel it! Though we can't really imagine what it will be. So we just wait.

In the meantime we have had our first fall of snow, and I wonder what Peep will do without her shelter and feed, and the warm coat we put on her sometimes.

So *please* write if you can. I long to hear what has been happening to the rest of the wild herd in Tachi's absence, and if you still worry about him being so far away.

Drop me a line (if your Aunt Scroghli isn't too busy).
With kind regards to all your family,

Your troubled English friend,
Kitty Jamieson

6

My Dear Friend Kitty,

Of course I received all your wonderful letters, but my Aunt
Seroghli was in Sverdlovsk, so there was no one here to read
them to me, or to write back. I wanted to give them to our
English teacher to read, but my mother thought that would be
impolite to you, so I waited for Aunt Seroghli to come back.
Now she is back, and sends you her greetings and asks your
permission to read some of your letters to her students (she
teaches diploma students). She would be very grateful, because
it would help friendly understanding between our two peoples,
and tell our young people so much about the way you live.

Everything you wrote surprised me, because I had imagined
Tachi would be in a little English park (the kind we read about)
with no open grasslands like ours. But Gritti (you remember
the zoologist) said that one of the reasons why you got Tachi
was the wonderful Reserve you have, and the similarity of
conditions, though not the weather. So I do not worry about
Tachi so much. But you describe everything so well that I can
picture Tachi waiting for a chance to get away.

But where will he go to, Kitty, if he does escape? That is
what worries me. I looked at a map of your little country, and
you have thousands of roads and villages everywhere. If he ever

does escape I think he will be in danger of being killed on a road. Or perhaps some farmer might shoot him as a dangerous animal. The one thing I know that he will *never* do is swim a river. As your grandfather said, our wild horses hate sheet water.

The herd is not the same since Tachi left. They seem to me to be very careless without him. But of course they are safe now, if the coming winter is not too hard. The Mongolian government has now made our mountains a Reserve for the wild horse, and next year they will begin to help the wild horses through the winter by cutting shelters in the hillsides, and putting down food where the herd will be able to find it if the winter is hard.

As for me: I am doing much better at school now, and my aunt says I do not day-dream so much since they took Tachi away. But I often lie awake at night thinking of him, and wondering how he feels so far away from home. Like you, I try to put myself in his place, and I know I would be very unhappy if I thought I would never see my own grasslands and mountains again. He must long to be back in his homeland.

I shall write again when Aunt Seroghli comes back from Ulan Bator, where she will post this letter.

With best wishes from all my family to you and to your wonderful grandfather and to Mrs Evans. My mother made Aunt Seroghli read all the parts about Mrs Evans again and again, and my mother kept shaking her head and nodding and sighing, 'Tttt, Tththt,' because she knows exactly what Mrs Evans was going through. My regards to Skip as well.

Your far-away friend,
Baryut
Pupil of the 4th Form

PS My aunt says she will send you a book which is a very simple grammar of our language, in English. I am going to study English very seriously now, and I will not be happy until some day I can read your letters and write my own replies. I enclose a photograph of myself taken last year sitting on my brother's new motor bike. I cannot really ride it, but I do know how to. On the left is my sister Miza, looking very worried because she thought I was actually going to ride off. Baryut

7

Dear Baryut,

This is going to be a very, very sad letter, so please get ready for it. In fact before you've even read a word of this letter I have to apologise for everything I write in it.

You've probably guessed what has happened. Tachi has gone, and he's taken Peep with him. I didn't write to you the moment it happened because none of us really believed it, not even Peter who was always saying it would happen. But it did happen. It just happened!

I'd better start at the beginning, otherwise all will be mess and confusion and huge splashy tears. You remember how I wrote that Peep was trying to get Tachi closer to the house, and we hoped it was a good sign! For ten days after that we didn't even see them, not even Peter, and just as we were beginning to worry again, they turned up practically on top of the mountain where Peter lives in the Crow's Nest. He saw them one clear day when the mountains were covered in snow. He couldn't believe his eyes.

'I don't see how they could have climbed this high,' Peter said on the radio. 'It's incredible.'

'Is there any fodder up there, any grazing?' Grandfather asked as if he wasn't at all surprised.

'I can't tell,' Peter said. 'But what does that crazy horse think he's doing up here?'

'Who knows?' Grandfather said. 'But what a horse!'

But I keep thinking of Peep, and I said, 'Poor Peep! Tachi is *forcing* her to follow him. He's threatening her . . .'

Grandfather became furious. 'I've told you before,' he said. 'Do *not* put the human mind into a horse's head.'

So Peter just watched them until they disappeared again, and once more we had to worry because the weather became bitterly cold and windy, and the rain was so freezing that it seemed to bore little holes in your face.

'Visibility nil,' Grandfather says every morning in that sort of weather.

So we did not expect to see either Tachi or Peep as long as it lasted. Peter, in his Crow's Nest, said he was living (dancing, probably!) in a little white cloud world of his own, because he was above the rain in a blue sky, while we were underneath it in a miserably grey, wet valley.

After weeks it cleared again, and once more we began to look seriously for Tachi and Peep. Grandfather said that Tachi was obviously teaching Peep to forage at night and hide by day. That was the usual way of the wild horse. But even the rangers couldn't find them, until one day Mr Selby (who lives in the cottage) said that he'd caught a sudden glimpse of Tachi and Peep lying down in a little hole in the hillside, sheltering from the wind. When they saw Mr Selby they immediately got up and galloped away.

So again we were relieved, and we were even getting used to them disappearing. We knew now that they were definitely hiding by day and feeding by night. So, when another two weeks passed without seeing them, we were not worried. But then another week went by, and still no sign of them, and this time we *did* begin to worry.

But what could we do?

Looking back on it, Grandfather blames himself for underestimating Tachi's character and determination. Or,

54

for leaving it too long before we called in the RAF helicopters. The rangers had walked over every possible nook and cranny of the Reserve on foot, and Mr Selby had ridden his pony in and out of all the valleys. Peter had used his powerful binoculars (about as big as a chair) and his telescopes, and he had even gone out onto the mountain as far as he could. Grandfather and I had searched every possible corner in our area, and even Mrs Evans would come into the study sometimes and try to look through the big binoculars.

'If you'd had any sense you would have put some food down around the house,' Mrs Evans said to Grandfather. 'That would have brought that pony home.'

Grandfather just snorted angrily, and they began a terrible quarrel. They were really very upset, and I suppose my silly, wretched face upset them too, although I tried never to look too gloomy when I was near them.

In any case there was no sign of the two horses, and finally Grandfather called the RAF Helicopter Rescue station at Newport and asked their help. We don't like helicopters over the Reserve, because they frighten the animals, but sometimes in bad weather we ask their help to get fodder to the wild goats on the steep slopes.

The RAF sent two helicopters and said we could have them for two days. One of the pilots asked me if I would like to go with them.

'Of course!' I said, and before he could change his mind I clambered up the steep metal ladder and off we went. I kept feeling as if I was on a flying plate (not a saucer). And that some giant was swinging the plate around his head. We went down the valleys, and over the mountains, tilted, and Grandfather and the others were looking everywhere with their binoculars.

After two days of searching we knew that Tachi and Peep were no longer in the Reserve. In fact on the second day Mr Selby reported that he had found a break in the wire fence, way over to the east of the mountains. It was almost dark, and we were all tired but Grandfather persuaded one of the helicopter pilots to take us to the spot. We got there in less than half an hour, just where the electric wire fence met an old solid stone wall, part of an ancient mine (a Celtic gold mine).

'It's not the wire fence, it's the wall that's down,' Mr Selby pointed out.

The place where the wire ended and the high old stone wall began was all kicked down. If you could see that wall, Baryut, you would wonder how even a bulldozer could have made such a hole in it. The big stones had been kicked and kicked, and some of the top stones were twenty yards away on the other side. It wasn't much of a hole, just enough for them to get through, but it was hard to believe that a horse, particularly a tiny horse like Tachi, could make such a gap.

'Incredible!' Grandfather said. 'He must have pounded away here for days and days. He must have kept at it, in that one place, for heaven knows how long.'

We looked at the stones that were on the other side, and some of them were covered in blood. So Tachi had obviously beaten at them until he bled.

'Probably cut his hoofs to pieces as well,' Mr Selby said.

'Probably,' Grandfather said unhappily.

By now it was dark and there was no point trying to search the other side. So we went back home in the helicopter and Grandfather had a difficult time persuading the RAF to lend us a helicopter for one more day so that we could search the hills outside the fence. He had to telephone all sorts of important people, but finally he was told that he could have a helicopter for the next morning and that was the limit.

'At least it will give us a bit of a chance,' Grandfather said.

I didn't think it would help, because I knew that Tachi would not waste time hanging around the Reserve. 'He's probably miles away by now,' I said to Grandfather.

'Going where?' he said irritably. 'Where do you think he's heading?'

'I don't know,' I said. 'But if he really wants to escape, Grandfather, he'll just go on and on.'

'I suppose you're right,' Grandfather said gloomily. 'Although Peep may slow him up a bit.'

From 5.30 next morning until 1.30 p.m. we searched all the surrounding hill farms from the air, and though we flew over many hill ponies and horses, it was easy to see that Tachi and Peep were not among them. Tachi had already changed his yellow summer coat for his thick reddish winter fur, but he was so unusual anyway that you could always pick him out.

When we flew back home that Sunday we were all very depressed, and even Peter (whom we had picked up and put down again in the Crow's Nest) said that life would never be quite the same up there without Tachi rampaging around in his wild search for something.

'Don't worry,' Grandfather insisted. 'He'll turn up.'

I don't think he will, and I said angrily to Grandfather that I was sure we would never see either of them again.

That night Grandfather came into my bedroom and read me a passage out of a book called *The Asiatic Wild Horse*, and it said that a wild horse named Tornado had once been found 120 kilometres away after it had escaped from Prague zoo.

'And that was not in a thickly populated country like ours,' Grandfather said, 'where he can be seen very quickly.'

I knew he was trying to cheer me up, but I also knew he was trying to cheer himself up. Next day (Monday) when I was at school he began to phone all the local police stations and all the local hill farmers around us. Finally he contacted the Chief Constables of all the surrounding counties and explained what had happened and asked them if their police would keep a look-out for the two horses. In fact he got on to all sorts of other organizations as well:

57

wild-life associations, ramblers clubs, land workers, farmers' organizations. He was on the phone all day, and by the time he went to bed that night I think he was sure that he had spread a huge net all over the neighbouring counties, so that sooner or later the two horses would be spotted.

That was exactly 23 days ago, Baryut, and there has been no word from anyone, anywhere. Not a word. Which is incredible. The two of them have just disappeared right off the map, and every time I say that, even to myself, the awful splashing begins. So all these disgusting smears you can see on this page are just me losing control. But I can't help it, even though it's silly.

But it's really Grandfather whom I feel sorry for, because he has not only lost his most valuable animal (the one he was waiting for ever since he came to the Reserve) but he's especially upset because 'this rare and wonderful little beast was entrusted to me by my friends, the Mongolian scientists,' he groans. 'And I was quite stupid. Stupid!' he keeps saying.

When I tell him not to be so upset, he says, 'But I under-estimated the real character of that horse, and his real intentions. Although I wish I knew what his real intentions were, even now. What does he think he's doing?'

So they've both gone, Baryut, and I don't know which one I miss most. We don't even know where to look any more. At one point Grandfather became so desperate that he took the Land Rover and went wandering all around Gloucester-shire and even as far away as Berkshire, asking farmers and villagers if they'd seen any sign of the two horses.

Have they fallen down some disused old quarry? Are they drowned in a river? Or even in the sea? Have they been killed by a farmer? Were they run over? Or captured? (Impossible with Tachi.) Or lost? (Where?) Or hurt? Or sick? That's all I can tell you except that we still haven't given up hope. We know that Tachi is a stubborn and determined horse.

But I'll end this now before I start getting depressed again. And I do apologize for everything, Baryut, and hope that you understand how badly we all feel.

Your very sad English friend,
Kitty Jamieson

PS I'll write the instant we hear something. I haven't the heart to send you any photographs of myself, because I don't suppose you'll want one now. Kitty

8

Dear Kitty,

Please do not let your grandfather blame himself for Tachi's disappearance, because Tachi was obviously determined to escape, no matter what precautions you took. That is his wild nature. So please tell your grandfather.

But I do not think Tachi will let any harm come to Peep. Horses are terribly loyal to each other when they pair off, and Tachi will fight anything that tries to harm her, although my aunt says he cannot fight weather or motor cars or accidents, can he? But I do not think he is dead. He is too clever to be dead.

So cheer up, and please send me the photographs. I would like to have them very much.

Your sympathetic friend,
Baryut

PS My aunt has found several books in Russian by the well-known Welsh writers Gwyn Thomas and Richard Llewellyn, which she will read to me. B.

9

Dear Baryut,

I couldn't write before, although it's months since I got your last letter (3 months 22 days). But I just didn't have the heart to write when there was nothing to report.

And now that there *is* something to report, I'm not very sure what it means. Anyway, after weeks and weeks of no news we began to get hundreds (really hundreds) of reports from all over Britain saying that Tachi and Peep had been seen. Some were from the police, some from wild-life enthusiasts, some from farmers or country people, and some from strangers who had heard about their disappearance. (One newspaper made a big joke of it and said 'Wild West horse lost in Britain'.) Grandfather seems to have done nothing else but answer the phone and rush off at a moment's notice to places as far away as Essex and Norfolk and even Scotland.

But no luck. Every single one of the reports was a false alarm. Only one woman had actually seen them. She runs a chicken farm not far from the Reserve, but she didn't know we were looking for Peep and Tachi until someone told her weeks later. She had obviously seen them the night they escaped. She had been awakened by her dogs barking. Thinking it was a prowling fox she went out with a shotgun and a torch. She flashed the torch on a bin which she kept bran in. She said she saw two strange animals stealing from the bin, so she fired. She thinks she missed. Then she realized that what she had been shooting at was a 'Shetland pony and a thoroughly misbegotten-looking animal disguised as a horse'. That's how she described Tachi.

Both horses immediately ran off into the darkness and

Mrs Jackson (the chicken farmer) said one of them was very lame, although she can't remember which one it was. She said she was sure she didn't cause its injuries, but she said it could hardly move.

Grandfather thought about it and said, 'Obviously Tachi. It must be the injuries he suffered when he battered down that wall.'

Though it was weeks later, we tried to find out where they might have gone to, but of course there was no more sign of them anywhere.

Then one morning Grandfather got a letter in French from a Monsieur Fanon, Deputy Keeper of the Bordeaux Zoo, asking him if it was possible that the wild Mongolian horse missing from our Reserve could somehow have reached France. Monsieur Fanon said that he had read of the disappearance of our wild horse in one of the French zoological journals. He thought he had better write to Grandfather because one day recently he had been speaking to the zoo's meat supplier from Le Havre (the French port), who said that he had seen a very strange, fuzzy-looking horse among a big herd of imported horses which were being taken to the slaughterhouse at Quillebeuf. Monsieur Fanon said that the meat supplier's description of the 'strange' horse fitted that of a Mongolian wild horse losing its winter coat. He said he had tried to find out more, but that was all the meat supplier knew.

'If you think there is any possible way your wild horse could have reached France,' Monsieur Fanon wrote, 'I will pursue my enquiries here. But only if you consider it a genuine possibility.'

When we got this letter Grandfather immediately sent Monsieur Fanon a telegram saying that there was absolutely no way he knew of that our wild horse could have reached France. But Grandfather also said that anything short of swimming the Channel was possible with this particular

horse. So he would be very grateful if Monsieur Fanon would pursue the enquiries anyway, while Grandfather himself looked into the possibility of it from this side.

So that's the latest news, Baryut. It's hopeful and yet awful. If it was Tachi (and Peep?) what on earth were they doing with horses being led to the slaughterhouse in France. (Horrible thought!) And was that the end of them? The slaughterhouse!

I just don't believe it. I refuse to.

We therefore wait now to see what Monsieur Fanon and Grandfather can find out. I don't know which I prefer: that they find out something, or that they find out nothing.

Mrs Evans sends you her warmest love. 'I've never seen anybody Mongolian,' she said the other day. 'What do they look like?' I then showed her your picture, and she said, 'It just goes to show, doesn't it.'

I finally enclose some photographs. There is one of all of us together. The one of Mrs Evans was specially taken in the photo-machine in Woolworth's in Newport. She really looks much nicer and more motherly than that, but the ones of Grandfather and me and Peep are not bad, especially Peep who looks like a neat little toy, doesn't she?

With hope in my heart, etc. etc. etc. etc. etc.!!!

Yours ever,
Kitty

PS Everybody here also sends special greetings to your Aunt Seroghli, who is so patient with us and writes such marvellous English. Much better than mine in fact. Has she ever been to England? We hope to see you all some day over here. Perhaps when we find Tachi and Peep again. Kitty

*　　*　　*　　*　　*

Dear Kitty,

I have not heard from you for a very long time, so I am still waiting anxiously to know whether the 'strange' horse in France going to the slaughterhouse was Tachi or not. I studied the atlas in our school library very closely, and I cannot imagine how he could have got to France. Being the wild horse he is, he would never have gone willingly into a ship. So how could it be he?

We have all been speculating ever since we received your letter. Everyone here has a different theory, including my father, grandfather, brothers, sister, Aunt Seroghli; and even my mother who says that we are all foolish to speculate because 'of course it is Tachi'. She says she already knows the real secret about Tachi, but she will not tell us what it is. My mother loves little mysteries, and she loves to tease us with them. But she says she will only tell us the secret about Tachi when the proper time comes. In the meantime, *nothing* will get it out of her.

I hope she is right. So please write if you have a moment.

With greetings to Mrs Evans, your grandfather, Peter in the Crow's Nest and Skip.

Yours fraternally,
Baryut

PS Your photographs are all in a special frame we found in one of our old boxes. The frame was lying forgotten for years. It is made of plaited horse-hair, and was once part of a religious article which of course we do not need any more. Don't you think a horse-hair frame is interesting? Baryut

*   *   *   *   *

Dear Baryut,

I apologise for not putting you out of your misery sooner, but all sorts of extraordinary things have been happening.

Sometimes I can't really believe anything. In fact every time I decided to sit down and write you the news so far, something else would turn up.

When Monsieur Fanon wrote to my grandfather and asked him if it was possible that Tachi had crossed to France (with Peep?), Grandfather decided to do a bit of detective work himself, using the methods of the famous Sherlock Holmes (our great detective, who died about a hundred years ago).

'Holmes always insisted that you must tackle the obvious first,' Grandfather said. 'So let us assume that Tachi *did* get to France, and that he must have arrived there with a herd of horses which had been shipped to France for slaughter. So let me see first of all if I can find out if there are such shipments of horses from England, and where they leave from, and where they send them.'

To cut a long story short, Grandfather went all over the south coast asking questions. He wrote dozens of letters and made endless phone calls, until finally he discovered that broken-down old horses really are shipped from England and Ireland to France and Belgium for slaughter. I came home from school one day (I am now top in geography ever since I got so fascinated with Mongolia, and I know a lot more about your country now), I came home and I found him on the floor of the study with all sorts of maps.

'Well,' he said, 'I think I can trace what might have happened. There is a horse dealer named Speck in Newbury who goes around the country with two big lorries buying up old nags and not-so-old nags: old milk horses and farm horses as well as perfectly healthy horses and moor ponies – all for slaughter. In fact some of the moorland farmers say that dozens of the wild moor ponies are simply stolen at night and taken off in lorries. So Mr Speck ends up with a herd of about 25 horses every month.'

'Every month!' I said. I was horrified. 'For slaughter?'

'Yes. Of course he doesn't tell anyone what he wants the horses for when he buys them. And he refused to talk to me. But I spoke to one of the horse-slaughterers in this country who supply horses for dogs' meat, and he swears that this fellow Speck from Newbury ships at least 500 horses a year to Belgium and France, and he says they're divided into two kinds: the old wrecks which are slaughtered for animal food (for cats, dogs and zoos), and the young and healthy ones that are killed for human consumption. Horse-meat is eaten in France and Belgium, and it's sold in a special type of butcher's shop called a *chevaline*. And they're the ones who get the young horse and pony meat.'

'You think that's what happened to Tachi and Peep?' I said.

'It's possible, Kitty. It's just possible. So you'd better start bracing yourself.'

He had to say it, and though I did not get upset for Grandfather's sake, I couldn't prevent one splash falling into the sugar bowl (we were having supper).

'But how would they ever get Tachi into a lorry, or on to a ship?' I asked Grandfather. 'They'd never be able to catch him or hold him down. He'd go mad.'

'You remember Mrs Jackson saying one of those two horses in her chicken yard was very lame?' Grandfather replied.

'Yes.'

'Perhaps Tachi was so badly hurt when he battered down the wall that in fact he was almost immobilized. He might have reached Exmoor or Dartmoor, and got caught with the other ponies. And, being so lame, he was easily roped in.'

'He would still fight.'

'I wonder. Perhaps he was cunning enough not to. Anyway, I'll send all the information I have to Monsieur Fanon, and we'll just have to wait for his reply to my questions.'

We didn't have long to wait because Monsieur Fanon had looked into it from his side, and he wrote back and told us what he had discovered. So here is Grandfather's translation of Monsieur Fanon's letter.

'I left Bordeaux last week to pursue the matter of the "strange and fuzzy-looking horse" in the herd waiting to be slaughtered at Quillebeuf. I took with me to Bordeaux the zoo's meat supplier who first told me about the strange horse. He normally collects the horse-meat for our tigers and lions from the Quillebeuf slaughterhouse every Friday. I questioned his friends at the slaughterhouse very closely, and they said that in fact there were two ponies: "the very ugly little stallion" and a "shaggy little gypsy (Shetland)". What is very significant, in view of your letter, Professor, is that the "ugly little stallion" was very lame, and the "gypsy" with him was a filly who seemed to stick very close to him. It seems likely, therefore, that this was your wild Mongolian horse, with his mate, the Shetland.'

That was only the first of Monsieur Fanon's letters, but by now Grandfather was sure that he was right. Tachi had been badly injured escaping from our Reserve, he had lain low for a while with the Exmoor ponies. Then he had been trapped and stolen with some of them. After that he must have been put on the horse ship near Rye and unloaded at Le Havre. He was still lame, and still accompanied by Peep, who was sticking by him so closely that they had been picked up together.

So far so good. But what happened at the Quillebeuf slaughterhouse? Here is Monsieur Fanon's second letter about that:

'When I made closer enquiries at the slaughterhouse nobody could remember the "strange and fuzzy-looking" little stallion or his companion ever actually reaching the slaughterer's hammer. The men who actually do the slaughtering remember the rest of that batch, but not one man among them said that he remembered any horse of the description we gave him. Yet I had traced the two ponies as far as the pen from which the slaughtermen normally took the horses one by one. The question is – would they have remembered any particular horse? I believe they would have, because they say that they know every feature and facial expression of every horse they must kill, much to their chagrin.

'I therefore came to the conclusion that neither the Mongolian nor the Shetland actually had ever gone further than the pen. So where were they? What had happened to them? Had they escaped? Or had someone taken them away? There were many questions to ask.

'I asked these questions, Professor Jamieson, of many people in the slaughter-yards and I finally discovered that in fact three ponies (not two) had escaped one night by doing something no horse had ever done before. One of them had somehow dug a hole under the low rails of the pen, and all three (the third was a piebald) had crawled under the rails, like a dog crawling under a fence.'

When Grandfather read that part out to me, we both shouted excitedly and at the same time, 'That's Tachi, all right!'

But to continue with Monsieur Fanon: 'The slaughter-yards are in a rather remote part of Quillebeuf, so I stood on the spot where the three ponies had crawled under the rails, and I tried to estimate which direction they would take. Knowing how clever the Mongolian is when it comes to hiding, I chose a route that led in and out of copses, along a river bed, and over some sugar-beet fields. So I followed the route and asked as many of the farmers and villagers as I could find if they had seen any sign of the escaped ponies. Eventually I found a village postman who had been out hunting early one morning and had seen the three ponies on the edge of a copse, about twenty kilometres from Quillebeuf. When the ponies saw him they began to flee, but one ("an ugly little pygmy" he called it) was only able to run on three legs because he was dragging one of his back legs. Even so, the postman said, they were able to move surprisingly fast, and they had disappeared into the woods by the time he reached the spot.'

Grandfather slapped his knees and said, 'So far so good.' He wanted to pack his bags and leave immediately for France. In fact we were both so happy by now that we were sure it was only a matter of time before we got both of our horses back again. However, I'd better continue with Monsieur Fanon:

'When I asked the postman if he had reported seeing the ponies, he said he had guessed that they had escaped from the slaughterhouse, and though he shot birds and rabbits for sport, he wasn't going to help anyone send a horse back to the slaughterhouse. So he told nobody about it. He said he wouldn't have told me except that he had heard that one of the horses was valuable, and that there might be a reward if it was captured.'

'Of course,' Grandfather said then. 'I didn't think of that. Of course there should be a reward. A hundred pounds, at least . . .'

Well, Baryut, to put everything else together quickly: Monsieur Fanon traced the three ponies for another 50 kilometres, heading east and south and obviously moving at night. Then he lost track of them completely. No sign at all beyond the River Lot. Nobody had seen them farther than that, and there were no reports of tracks or droppings.

'All I could do, after a vain search,' Monsieur Fanon said, 'was to alert our National Gendarmerie in as wide an area as possible, and then return to my duties at Bordeaux. I have written to professors and *gardes champêtre* in the areas of Aix en Provence, Lyon, Avignon, Arles, Nimes and Vaison la Romaine, asking them to watch out for our three travellers. I trust, Professor, that this will help. In any case I will be delighted to see you, and to give you any help I can. I will also be glad to accompany you to the river where they were last seen.'

That's all the news so far, Baryut. They are both alive,

even though Tachi is hurt. But Grandfather says his leg must be improving daily if he is able to move so far and so fast. And now they have that third pony – the piebald.

'Tachi is obviously collecting a herd as he goes,' Grandfather said and laughed about that. In fact I haven't seen him so happy for a long time. He hasn't been laughing much since Tachi and Peep first disappeared, but now he's pulling my hair again, and slapping his knees and saying, 'Marvellous horse! Amazing animal.'

He is off to France tomorrow to pick up the search. I begged and begged him to let me go with him, but he won't let me miss school, even for a week, although I've been doing very well lately, particularly in English, geography, history and French. I wish it was Mongolian though, instead of French. I try to study the grammar your Aunt Seroghli sent, but unless I can say things out loud to someone, I can't learn. So I really need you and your Aunt Seroghli here to listen to me and help me and to laugh at my mistakes. I tried it on Mrs Evans, but she laughed so much at the Mongolian words I was trying to say that I had to laugh too, and we both ended up as hopeless jellies. Mrs E. thinks you are all terribly clever to be able to speak Mongolian, and she keeps shaking her head and saying, 'It just goes to show, doesn't it.'

That's all for now. I'm quite exhausted. I'm sitting up in bed, and my fingers are stiff . . . writing awful . . . Skip keeps chasing cats in his sleep and making funny, squeaking little barks. So goodbye for now,

Your very sleepy but happy friend,
Kitty Jean Jamieson
(my full name)

PS If you send me a record of one of your Mongolian pop singers, I'll send you back one of ours, Tom Jones, or the Rolling Stones or whoever you like. Kitty

10

My Dear Kitty,

Thank you very much for finally 'putting me out of my misery' about Tachi and Peep. That is a very funny expression when translated in Mongolian, and I could not stop laughing. In Mongolian we say 'thank you for leading me back to the water'. But I was sure that Tachi and Peep would never end up in the slaughterhouse.

I only hope that Tachi has not injured himself permanently. With horses, leg injuries are usually fatal. Sometimes a wild horse with a broken or damaged leg manages to hobble around for a little while, but eventually it gets so weak that it collapses and cannot get up. Then it dies. So I hope Tachi is not in that situation. If it was only his hoofs that were injured then he will probably be all right.

I would like to tell you, Kitty, that you are now very famous in our district. Everyone now knows about your letters, and everybody in our collective comes to sit around in our tent (it is summer) to hear Aunt Seroghli read them out in Mongolian. It takes hours, because everybody discusses and argues about everything you have said or written. The old people just grunt or say 'Tch Tchh!', but everybody else has a theory. My mother loves your letters, and she just nods as if she already knew everything that was going to happen.

She still refuses to tell us her famous 'secret' about Tachi, even though I begged Aunt Seroghli to get it out of her. One night I heard my father and my mother laughing, and I knew it was about the way she teases us. She loves to tease. But I will get it out of her sooner or later.

Among the people who have also listened attentively to your letters are the visiting zoologists from Ulan Bator, who had heard from your grandfather that Tachi was missing, but did not know the details. They even took notes of what you said in your letter.

'Kitty should also think of becoming a zoologist, like you,' Aunt Seroghli said to me.

The zoologists keep coming to see the wild herd, and now we have found a dozen special routes up the mountains to the five look-out places, which the scientists can use without disturbing the herd. I spent all my last holidays helping our friend Gritti find all these new routes through the mountains. He's a real horse-finder now.

Meantime the herd goes on living safely in our mountains, unaware of all the interest they are inspiring. The final count of them was 26, but I think there are 5 more horses somewhere. When I first saw the herd I counted 35, including the 4 that were taken away. That should leave 31 not 26. So I secretly look for the missing 5, and one day I am sure I will find them.

As for Tachi; we still wait anxiously for news that you have recaptured him. What sort is the third horse? Tachi obviously thinks he can establish his own wild herd, even in the mountains of Europe. But Gritti says it is not as funny as it sounds, because wild horses roamed the whole land mass of Europe and Asia for many thousands of years, moving from Europe to Asia and from France to China, as if it were all their territory.

But we still miss him in the herd. They still lack a good guide and a future master stallion who is a clever and determined horse. Some of the other young stallions are beginning to challenge the old one, but they are not nearly as sharp or intelligent or as clever or brave as Tachi.

Please, therefore, write the moment you catch him.

Your friend,
Baryut

PS My Aunt Seroghli says that reading your letters, and translating everything I tell her, has improved her English very much. 'Why do you not write to Kitty yourself and tell her?' I

said. 'Or add a little note?' But Aunt Seroghli says it would spoil our letters if she put herself into them, so she simply asks me to thank you for all the help you have given her. B.

*   *   *   *   *

Dear Baryut,

Another gap in this correspondence, I know, but I'm aching all over at the moment because I fell down the side of the valley where I used to go with Peep. I was day-dreaming and looking for larks' nests (not to touch of course, but simply to see) and I slipped and tumbled a long way down the slope, which means that I'm bruised all over. I did not think I'd ever stop.

But first things first, as Grandfather says. You will remember that Grandfather went to France, sure that he would bring Tachi back with him. But he spent two whole weeks looking for tracks or traces, and it was only in the last two days that he found out which direction the three horses had taken. Even so, he couldn't find out where they had gone, and he had to return home very disappointed.

'I wouldn't have thought it possible,' he said, 'that three horses, one of them wild, could disappear so completely into the French countryside. Obviously it's Tachi's doing. And obviously they're still hiding by day and moving by night. But I still don't know how he does it.'

Grandfather keeps stamping around, asking himself angry questions and drumming the tips of his fingers together and pulling his hair and arguing with himself.

'What we really need,' he said yesterday, 'is a horse detective. But since we can't afford *any* sort of a detective, I have had to leave it in the capable hands of Monsieur Fanon.'

Grandfather says that Monsieur Fanon looks like a little terrier. 'He's only about five feet two inches tall, and so quick and alert that I could hardly keep up with him. When he starts questioning people you'd think it was a life and death matter for everybody. He won't give up, even when people think they don't know anything. He just gives them another mental shake, like a terrier with a rat, and he gets something else out of them. And of course he's dying to catch up with Tachi.'

So everything we know now comes from our new friend Monsieur Fanon, who thinks there is some sort of purpose or direction in what Tachi is doing. I don't know what he means. Perhaps you can discover what he's saying, Baryut, when you read his full report. So here it is:

'The wild horse does not seem to be moving in a straight line. He zig-zags his direction, like a sailing boat tacking back and forth in order to go in a straight line. He therefore has a direction; and I discovered, for instance, that he went steadily south and east and arrived eventually in the Camargue, which is, as you know, one of the largest nature reserves in the south of France, as well as being the only place in Europe where there are herds of domestic horses running wild. Also the famous Camargue ponies. It is dry and sandy and swampy – or part of it is. But a lot of it is the sort of salty flatland the Mongolian wild horses like.

'It was in the middle of the Camargue that a herder's son actually caught sight of the three horses. And if he had known then what they really were, we would have captured them by now. But they looked at a distance so like the Camargue ponies, that he didn't think anything of them at first. This boy was one of the local herders who look after a remote corner of the Camargue, where the dry marsh meets the wide water of one of the *etangs* (ponds). For several weeks, perhaps a month even, the boy kept seeing these "strange Camargue ponies" mixed in with the various groups of his own herd. But he could never get near them or see them long enough, to decide who they belonged to.

'But one day the boy was told to bring in four young

stallions, and when he went into the marshes to get behind the herd, he saw an extraordinary fight between what he called "a fierce little ape of a pony" and one of the full-sized Camargue horses which was considerably bigger than the little pony he was fighting. In other words, it was your wild Mongolian pony fighting a Camargue horse.

'The boy told me that he had never seen anything like that fight. Camargue horses are renowned for their ferocity. But the "little ape" simply lashed the Camargue stallion terribly, he said, and even refused to let him escape, or call off the contest as Camargue stallions do among themselves when one is the obvious victor. The wild Mongolian was obviously fighting to defend his little harem (Peep and the piebald), but he was also fighting to the death, and the Camargue horse was soon helpless. He was eventually brought down by the Mongolian, who was about to finish him off with his front hoofs when the boy caught up with him.

'At this point the wild horse turned on the boy and his mount, and charged them. He bit the horse and would have attacked again if the boy had not used his big whip, which probably surprised the Mongolian, who only then galloped off. And that was the last time the boy saw them.

'Unfortunately I wasted all that week in the Camargue hoping I could find them. I spent night after night with the gypsies there, the horsemen, the villagers. But the Mongolian and his little herd had gone.

'The next report I had came from the Gendarmerie at Grasse, which is about 200 kilometres to the east. A linesman attending the high tension cables, which are strung through the mountains, had seen three ponies playing for hours in a clearing in one of the pine forests. But when I reached Grasse two days later I was told that all this had happened three weeks before. So again I was weeks behind.

'Finally, I had another report from an army post on the Italian border, near Sospel.

'One of the officers in the army post said that he and two of his soldiers had seen three small horses crossing a very difficult slope along the frontier. The officer said that the soldiers had fired half a dozen shots at them to see if they could calculate the range of their automatic rifles. But when the horses heard the noise, one of them simply went mad, galloping up the slope and down again, urging the other two along with pushes and excited nudges. The officer thinks that one of the horses actually tried to run in an opposite direction, but the angry one got up on his hind legs and pawed the air all around the laggard, and they all disappeared into a clump of cork oak trees on the Italian side.

'Of course I shall pursue my enquiries as far as I can, Professor, but I can't do much personal investigation in Italy. The border is my official limit. I shall contact as many of my colleagues in Italy as I can, and I hope you will do the same. The one factor that seems to help is the deliberate direction the wild horse seems to be taking. Please let me know if you find out anything yourself from our Italian colleagues.'

And that, Baryut, is all the news we have so far from Monsieur Fanon. Grandfather is looking up maps and international reference books to see which professors or zoologists might be able to help in Italy.

But my fingers now feel as if they've been writing with a thick nail on wood. I can type now, but not fast enough. In any case I always seem to be galloping ahead of myself, so typing would be too slow.

Mrs Evans said to me yesterday, 'If your mind had been in your body, instead of ten miles ahead of you, you wouldn't have fallen down that hill and hurt yourself.'

I suppose she's right. I'm quite hopeless. I should have been asleep hours ago. So goodnight!

Yours in haste,
Kitty

*   *   *   *   *

Dear Kitty,

You will be pleased to hear that we have finally persuaded my mother to tell us her mysterious secret about Tachi. When Aunt Seroghli was reading your last letter, my mother was sitting there nodding her head as usual and saying 'Ah hah!' or 'Huh, huh!' as if she knew everything in it already. This made my grandfather so angry that he stopped Aunt Seroghli reading.

'Kera (my mother's name),' he said, 'you should not keep any secret from us. If you already know everything that is happening to the horse, which you seem to do, you must tell us how you know. Otherwise we will have to think badly of you.' My grandfather is very old (in fact he's really my great-grandfather) and he still thinks in the old way. So he is very superstitious, and is always upset by mysteries and predictions and secret knowledge. I think he is afraid of them.

So my mother, who did not wish to be impolite or upset Grandfather, apologised, and told him the truth.

'It's very simple, Bab (grandfather),' she said seriously to him, although her eyes were twinkling. 'Our wild horse is on his way home.'

'Impossible!' we all said.

'He is on his way home,' my mother repeated. 'He has set out to return to his own mountains. That is all I know, Bab. And that is why I know that he will never stop or pause or allow anything to get in his way. So do not be upset. That is all I know.'

78

Of course there was an uproar from everybody. What a discussion it began. And this time the map of the whole world was opened out on the mat and everybody crowded around it. When we showed my mother that if Tachi was on his way home he would have to cross all Europe and Asia, from the Atlantic to the Pacific, right across the world, thousands of kilometres, my mother was not at all impressed, and she said again very firmly:

'Our wild horse is on his way home!'

Can you believe that, Kitty?

I must say that once the idea is put into one's head it is very difficult to get rid of it. Yet I dare not even think of it. I have not asked Gritti what he thinks yet.

In any case my mother's teasing is not over. I am sure she is thinking up some new mystery. I have been learning to swim in the new reservoir they have built on our river. I did not know that pushing yourself through water was really a problem of hydraulics. That is what my brother says and he is studying to be an engineer. But he cannot swim either, even though he knows all about hydraulics.

Let me know what your grandfather thinks. I will not say a word about what I think until I hear from you and from him.

Affectionately,
Baryut

PS Do you play chess? Last week I was playing with Gritti while we were lying down watching the herd, and he suggests that you and I exchange some Anglo-Mongolian chess problems. B.

*   *   *   *   *

Dear Baryut,

When I read your letter to Grandfather, and when I read out your mother's sensational idea about Tachi, Grandfather slapped his knees and said:

'Amazing woman! Of course she's right. Of course the wild horse is heading for home. I suspected it myself, but because I was being scientific about it I didn't want to admit it. But Baryut's mother went straight to the point.'

Incredible as it seems, Baryut, that does seem to be the answer!

'You will even notice,' Grandfather said, 'that Tachi seems to be taking the best possible route. He probably has all the instinct of his horse ancestors, who once roamed freely across the vast expanse of Europe and Asia.'

'But how long would it take him to reach his mountains?' I asked Grandfather, still finding it difficult to believe.

'Who knows?' he said. 'One year. Two. Possibly more.'

So that is Grandfather's answer, Baryut. He believes it. And like you we will get out our maps of the world and we will try to see the route he will take. In the meantime I don't know whether to hope that Tachi actually avoids everybody for a whole year and finally reaches his home in your mountains, or whether to hope that he is caught very soon and brought back to us with Peep.

Of course I keep thinking of Peep and the piebald with him. They are both tame horses. And the way that Tachi is going about it they'll probably drop dead with exhaustion long before they reach Mongolia.

Anyway, Grandfather has written to the zoos and the professors in the universities in Turin, Milan, Venice and Trieste. He has also written to Monsieur Fanon and asked him if he agrees with your mother. Grandfather is sure Monsieur Fanon was really thinking the same thing all the time.

Which do you hope for, Baryut? That Tachi reaches his

mountain home? Or that he is caught and returned to us? And what about Peep? I keep thinking and worrying about her all the time.

Until something happens – though heaven knows what, I remain,

Your old friend,
Kitty J.

PS I can't play chess, but Grandfather says he will teach me. Mrs Evans thinks I have enough to do with my homework and school, but Grandfather says, 'Nonsense'.

PPS I think I really do want Tachi to reach his home in the mountains. But I don't know what I want Peep to do. Anything, so long as she isn't lost or hurt or left alone in some strange country. K.

I I

Dear Baryut,

I can't tell you what a problem it has been to keep track of Tachi and Peep and the piebald pony as they try desperately to keep going east. We have received all kinds of strange reports from all sorts of people in Europe, and when we finally had them all translated from French, Italian and German, I had to spend hours in Grandfather's study sorting them all out. The result is that we know now that they have had at least three terrible adventures, one after the other.

It's really Tachi that causes it. He obviously won't stop for anything. And we know now that he has been very badly injured again, and might even be dying. But because he still won't stop for anything at all, we don't know where it will all end.

The first trouble they had was in Italy. It was Monsieur Fanon who told us what happened there. He said he was allowed by his chiefs at the Bordeaux Zoo to go on into Italy, because they wanted to know how a wild animal like Tachi managed to survive and disappear in the middle of highways and farms and cities and towns. Monsieur Fanon said it was easy enough to see how Tachi crossed France. He just kept to the wild parts of the Alpes Maritimes mountains. But what would the three ponies do in Italy, which is thick with villages and roads, and full of people who are not going to allow stray horses to wander about?

So Monsieur Fanon first traced the route they took in Italy by questioning all the lorry-drivers he could find. Some of them had seen mysterious animals near the roads at night. And by following what they said, he traced the three horses to an Italian gypsy camp near Verona, which is half-way across northern Italy.

'Nobody knows exactly when it happened,' Monsieur Fanon said, 'but believe it or not the gypsies actually captured the wild horse and kept him.'

He said that the gypsies were water-carriers who moved around the country hiring themselves out to villagers and farmers to carry water to fruit trees, vines, vegetable plots, gardens or even to village houses. They used donkeys and horses and they lived in the fields in lorries and battered old caravans, and they had all sorts of other animals, goats, dogs and even a monkey.

Anyway, Baryut, the gypsies saw the three stray horses hiding in a wood near Verona. The gypsies said the horses were obviously trying to find a way around a big canal. They decided to catch them, and what they did was to arrange some trip-wires on one of the paths they had seen the horses use. Then they waited one night until the horses appeared, and they panicked them by flashing torches and beating kettles.

Peep and the piebald ran straight into the trip-wires and went down. But Tachi seemed to guess where the wires were, and he jumped over them and got away. But Peep and the little piebald were caught.

The gypsies then put Peep and the piebald into a sort of rough corral, fenced with rope, thinking they would be safe enough there. But the next night Tachi came back and tried to kick the rope-fence down. The gypsies ran out and tried to catch him, but whenever they got near him he attacked them. They were absolutely amazed. They had never seen a horse like this one, and Tachi actually got into the corral and got Peep out. Then he went back to get the little piebald, who didn't seem to want to go. So Tachi began kicking and butting her to force her to flee.

Seeing that they were about to lose all three horses the gypsies managed to lasso the piebald with a rope. But Tachi came back and attacked the men holding the rope. Unfortunately the gypsies were expecting him this time, and one of them hit Tachi hard on the forehead with a hammer and stunned him.

Ugggh! I can hardly bear to write it, Baryut. It must have been awful.

But Monsieur Fanon says that horse-gypsies know how to do it so that it doesn't seriously hurt the horse. In any case Tachi was knocked out, and the piebald and Peep escaped, leaving Tachi senseless on the ground.

When Tachi finally came to he was lying in a barbed-wire enclosure, tied by his legs, and the first thing the gypsies did to him when he came to was to throw a bucket of cold water over him. And they went on throwing water over him every time he tried to get up and attack them.

The piebald had finally managed to run off, as if she was

glad to escape from Tachi. But Peep stuck by Tachi. Every night she would come back to the barbed-wire fence and whinny and stamp her feet. Of course the gypsies tried to catch her again, but by now Peep was very clever at evading capture and she galloped off into the darkness.

(Poor Peep! But I'm so glad, Baryut, that she stuck by Tachi and refused to desert him.)

The gypsies tried their best to tame Tachi, but they discovered that they dared not untie his legs completely, even when he was up on his feet. They knew he would charge them, or might even try to jump the barbed-wire fence. They then tried to put baskets on his back (they carried the big water skins in baskets), but he bit and kicked and rolled over and smashed anything they put on him.

The gypsies were still throwing water on him, hoping to wear him out, but also because they wanted to get him used to being wet, which would be his fate if they trained him as a water carrier. So they were not being cruel. But they had to move on. So they tied Tachi up like a chicken and put him in one of the trucks and drove away. Fortunately they could not carry all the other goats and donkeys and dogs and horses in the trucks, so most of the other animals moved on foot. And Peep followed them at night at a safe distance, still refusing to desert Tachi.

This time the gypsies camped by a river. They built the barbed-wire corral again and dragged Tachi into it and left him loose there with his back legs loosely hobbled together. But one night when it was raining, and when the gypsies were all inside their caravans rather than outside, they heard a horse scream with pain. They rushed out, and they were in time to see Tachi staggering off with part of the barbed-wire fence hanging from his chest, dragging two posts with him.

By the time they got lights they could see Tachi kicking and trying to free himself from that awful barbed wire. They could also see that the ropes they had tied around his legs were broken. But they didn't try to reach him because they were sure that he would not get far dragging the barbed-wire. In fact they were afraid of making it worse, because he was bleeding and limping very badly. Even so, whenever they did try to come near him he turned on them and tried to bite and kick. So they just let him go on dragging the barbed-wire for about half a kilometre, while they followed and waited for him to collapse with the pain, or catch the wire in something.

Finally he came to a deep ditch that ran alongside a dirt road, and the gypsies were sure they would catch him here. But not Tachi. It must have caused him terrible pain, but he got up a little speed and actually jumped the ditch with the posts and barbed wire wrapped around him. In fact the ditch was so deep under him that the whole tangled mess suddenly fell off him, and he stumbled up the other side, no longer hung with wire and posts. The last the surprised gypsies saw of Tachi, he was staggering down the dusty road with Peep. The gypsies were all on foot, and by the time they got their horses to chase him, Tachi and Peep had completely disappeared in the darkness. And that was the last the gypsies ever saw of either of them.

The little piebald was caught thirty kilometres away and handed back to the gypsies who turned her into a water carrier. Better than the slaughter yards, I suppose. But I'm so glad that Peep was loyal to Tachi and escaped with him.

That was the end of their first adventure, and it left Tachi terribly injured and almost unable to walk. But he would not stop moving. He just kept heading for home, Baryut, going east. Always east. In fact we don't know how he managed to keep going at all, but, believe it or not, he and Peep crossed Italy and got as far as Austria before they ran into trouble again.

This time it was with a forester with a gun.

I suppose it was all just bad luck, but there was an old man living on the mountain borders of Italy and Austria who was a shepherd. He looked after a flock of goats and sheep, and because there is not much frontier control in the mountains up there, the old man would take his flock back and forth across the frontiers of Italy and Austria without anyone bothering him. He was an Austrian, but half his family lived on the Italian side. That's the way it is in those mountains. So the people think of the mountains as theirs, and they know all the difficult and secret paths across them.

One night the old man was taking his flock into Austria across a very difficult part of the mountains, going east, and he had a strong feeling that he was being followed by some sort of wild animal. Later on he told Professor Schmidt (who eventually wrote and told Grandfather everything we know about it) that he didn't know what kind of wild animal it could be. It was sixty years since there had been wild bears in the district, and all the wild pigs had been killed. There were wolves, though, and by the way the dogs behaved he thought it was a wolf. But the only thing he really knew for sure was that his flock was being followed in the darkness, and that the animals were as nervous and as scared as he was.

He hurried his flock in the darkness, and he said he only wished that they didn't have bells around their necks, because the clanging of the little bells in the mountains made it impossible to hear if he was still being followed.

When he finally did see the wild animals following him it was on the crest of the mountain pass. He heard a long eerie sound, he said, and when he looked up on the mountain top he saw two shaggy, wild beasts in the moonlight, but he didn't know what they were. Remember, Baryut, that both Tachi and Peep are very small, and there aren't many horses that size in that part of Europe. They were not only shaggy and wild, but no doubt Tachi was waving his head about. In fact the old shepherd thought they were giant wolves, and he was so frightened for his flock and for himself (and I don't blame him) that he left the flock and

ran down the alpine slope to a little hut where an Austrian forest guard (called a *Förster*) lived.

'Wolves!' the old man shouted when the *Förster* asked him what was the matter. (It was 1 o'clock in the morning.) 'Bring your gun, *Förster*,' he said. 'But be quick, because I had to leave the flock with the dogs.'

The *Förster* didn't really believe the old man, although there were times when wolves from Italy had been driven by hunger to that part of Carinthia, and even a man was not always safe from them. But he took his gun and hurried out in the darkness after the old shepherd.

The shepherd expected when he got back to find his flock in a panic – with half a dozen wolves among them. But he found them huddled together in a hollow, with the dogs whining nervously. But no wolves, and no sign of the real culprits – Tachi and Peep.

But the *Förster* also knew by the frightened behaviour of the sheep and the dogs that there was a wild animal somewhere, so now he believed the old man, and began to hunt the mountainside for wolves, while the old man moved his flock forward again, hurrying to get them safely out of the mountain pass.

I asked Grandfather why Tachi would want to follow the shepherd and his flock, and Grandfather thinks that it was Tachi's wild instinct to follow sheep and goats through a difficult mountain pass, because they always knew the best way, and wild animals often follow each other like that. So Tachi and Peep went on following the flock at a distance, and when the *Förster* eventually caught sight of them in the moonlight he too was puzzled by their appearance. He didn't know what they were, but with his *Förster's* instinct he decided to treat them as dangerous.

He waited with his rifle above a big rock where the passage through the mountains passed a very narrow place. The moment the two 'wild animals' appeared he aimed at one and pulled the trigger. But just as he fired, the 'wild beast' leapt forward as if he knew he was being fired at. The shot missed. The *Förster* shot at them again, but the two horses ran down the slope and plunged right through the flock of sheep, scattering them in panic. Then the two of them disappeared into the pine forests that covered the hill-side.

And that was the last the *Förster* and the shepherd saw of them.

Next day the *Förster* reported his adventure with the two 'wild animals' to the Austrian forestry officers in Lienz, and one of the officers wrote out a long report of what the shepherd and the *Förster* had seen. Eventually it went to Professor Schmidt in Vienna, who went and spoke to the *Förster* and the shepherd, and then wrote Grandfather everything they said. But the forestry officer's report also went to a Dr Shultz of the Vienna University Zoological Society, and that's how the third adventure began.

Dr Shultz knew immediately what the 'wild animals' were, and he set out like a hunter to track them down. He said in his letter to Grandfather that he intended to shoot Tachi with a dart gun, the same kind as your scientists used on Tachi before. But since then Grandfather has told me that it isn't the best way to capture wild animals, because only an expert marksman can hit the animals in the right place. Men who are not good marksmen often hit the animal in the wrong place, and the dart goes in too deep, or sometimes the animal is brought down in such a way that it breaks its leg or even its neck. So I got very upset and began to make a bit of a fuss when I read that Dr Shultz was going to hunt them with a dart gun. Grandfather tried to calm me down. What was I crying about? No harm would come to Tachi. He wasn't going to break his neck, etc. etc.

'Even if he doesn't break his neck,' I yelled, 'what happens to Peep once they've captured Tachi? They won't care what happens to her.'

I knew it was silly, but I didn't like the sound of Dr Shultz. Maybe he would leave Peep to fend for herself, or he might have her put away.

Mrs Evans heard me making a fuss and told Grandfather that as usual he was being inconsiderate and thoughtless. Then they began quarrelling and saying 'Nonsense' to each other, so I had to stop them, which made me feel better.

But Grandfather was also worried, because he suddenly remembered that he knew Dr Shultz. He remembered that Dr Shultz had spent many years in East Africa, and that there was always something of the secret hunter, rather than the scientist, in him.

'I don't mean that he likes to kill,' Grandfather said. 'But he enjoys the chase as hunters do, and chasing a wild horse across Europe may be what he is really interested in, rather than recapturing Tachi for conservation and scientific purposes.'

The first report we got from Dr Shultz said that he had finally caught up with Tachi and Peep a few kilometres from the Hungarian border with Austria. Tachi had gone right across Austria, and was now almost in Eastern Europe. So he was still going east. Dr Shultz said that he had tracked them over the most extraordinary zig-zag route (remember what Monsieur Fanon said). But one thing was clear – they seemed to be avoiding climbing any high mountains. They always looked for a way through the valleys.

'That's obviously because Tachi is still suffering from the wound he got from the barbed wire,' Grandfather said. 'Or perhaps the *Förster* wounded him with his rifle.'

So Dr Shultz went on hunting them like wild game, and he finally saw them one evening after picking up their tracks in a soft, muddy valley. He knew all day he was getting close to them because the hoof-prints were fresh, and so were the droppings. When he finally caught sight of them through his field glasses it was almost evening, and they were lying down in a corner of a neglected apple orchard in a mountain valley near the Austrian-Hungarian border.

Dr Shultz said he had to use all his African training to get near them. It was not only a matter of following all the simple rules of hunting, he said, such as keeping down-wind and never showing himself, it was also a matter of moving so quietly that he could get fifty or sixty metres from them. A dart gun is not accurate further than that, as you know.

He said it took him an hour to move only 100 metres. But he had a good look at Tachi as he got closer to him. Tachi had his October coat on, and it was thick and patchy. His tail and upright mane were very long. But Tachi himself looked very ill and weak. Peep, on the other hand, looked in perfect health. Her coat was thick and shiny. And it was Peep who seemed to be on guard, while Tachi was asleep on his feet.

Dr Shultz thought that this was the perfect moment, because mares are never as alert as stallions. Only another 100 metres and he would be close enough to fire the dart. But Peep was already restless, and it took Dr Shultz half an hour to move only 50 metres. Then, when he finally got near enough, he realized he had forgotten to cock the gun. As he carefully pulled back the bolt of the rifle, there was a slight click. That was all. But it was enough to awaken Tachi, who swung around and fled in a second.

Unfortunately Dr Shultz had time to aim, and he fired.

Dr Shultz was certain that he hit Tachi in the left shoulder with the drugged dart. Even in the darkness he saw Tachi jump. But then they both galloped off through the deserted orchard.

Dr Shultz didn't hurry, because he knew Tachi could not get far. He would certainly fall senseless before he had gone 50 metres. The nearest village was only 3 kilometres away, so Dr Shultz said he would hire a truck there to carry Tachi out. He also had a rope with him to tie Tachi's legs while he was unconscious. So he began to follow their tracks through the orchard, using a torch now to find the way because it was getting dark. But the doctor was surprised to see that Tachi had not collapsed after 50 metres, or even after 100 metres, which is the usual effect the darts have. Yet he was absolutely certain that he had hit Tachi.

In fact Tachi never collapsed at all. Why?

Dr Shultz said he didn't know why. And though he spent most of the night and the next day searching, there was no sign of either Tachi or Peep. He couldn't even find any more trace of their tracks, because above the orchard the mountainside was hard and dry and very steep, and this time, by some extraordinary effort, they had obviously climbed the mountains to escape.

And that, Baryut, was the last report we had from Dr Shultz. Tachi had a drugged dart in him and was climbing the mountain. And if you still ask (as everybody else does) why the drugged dart didn't seem to affect him, Grandfather says that his thick coat may have protected him. But I don't know. Perhaps he just kept going long enough to find a good place to hide in. Perhaps he got up on the mountain and died up there. Perhaps Dr Shultz killed him, and then said he'd disappeared, although Grandfather gets angry when I say that.

But that's all we know of them until now.

So if Tachi is not dead on some lonely Austrian mountain top, they must be pressing on. Grandfather has written to all the zoological societies in Hungary to warn them to look out for our two horses.

But I wonder, Baryut, how long they can go on, even if Tachi is able to walk. Now I hope that someone does catch them, so that Tachi can get help.

Otherwise . . .

Mrs Evans is calling me to help her with the mixed pickles she is making. I smell hot vinegar.

We all send our love and affection, Baryut, and promise to let you know, the moment we hear anything more.

Your usual friend,
Kitty

PS Nothing to add. Must hurry. I love Mrs E.'s pickles. K.

12

Dear Kitty,

When Aunt Seroghli read your letter to us we all said that Tachi ought to be captured and stopped, so that he did not kill himself and Peep too.

Even so, Kitty, we can't help admiring Tachi. My father keeps shaking his head and saying, 'That is a true Mongolian horse! He will keep on going until he drops dead, rather than give up. Only a Mongolian horse is like that.'

But my mother reminded him that Peep is not a Mongolian horse, and that she also keeps going. And my mother said, 'Perhaps only a little English horse would be so loyal to its mate.'

In any case I cannot believe that Tachi is dead. He would never give up like that. He is alive somewhere. But where?

In the meantime, we keep looking at the map and hoping for the best. Everybody here sends you their love. And a special greeting, as usual, from my mother to Mrs Evans.

Your old friend,
Baryut

PS Nothing to add either. It is not a very happy time, is it? I do not seem to be able to say anything more. B.

13

Dear Baryut,

It's hard to believe. In fact it's incredible. But after four months we finally got some news from Hungary, and Grandfather immediately caught a plane to Budapest. He's back now. But I must tell you straight away that he hasn't brought back Tachi or Peep with him, worse luck. What he did bring back was a long letter which explains everything that happened to them.

It is from a Hungarian girl named Kato Kosuth. And because it is best that you read it all for yourself, I'm putting in a photocopy of the translation we had made at Swansea University. So here it is:

Dear Kitty Jamieson (she spells my name Jamanson),

Your grandfather told me all about your pony, Peep, and the wild horse, Tachi. So I write to you because you will understand how I feel about all the strange things that have been happening, and how I came to get involved with both your ponies.

I am Hungarian and I live with my parents and my name is Kato Kosuth. But I do not live in a house, because my family are part of a village fair which travels all over Hungary, summer and winter, and includes all kinds of things such as calliopes (merry-go-rounds), little big-dippers, ring-the-prize, electric swings, target shooting, dancing, acrobats, strong men, and my family's part which is performing horses (two). And also pony rides for children.

Our fair is very old, and my family have been part of it for hundreds of years. We have always done it. Our fair is also very popular in Hungary, and villagers write to us every year begging us to go to them on feast days or religious holidays or national holidays, but we have our own regular route and find it very difficult to oblige everybody.

These days it is a good life because we do not have to pay high prices for everything, or high taxes, and we are not treated as gypsies. We are allowed to go everywhere, providing we do not allow the fair to get dirty or dangerous. So everything is bright and clean, and we actually have a school, which I attend four days and two nights a week. I will learn English next year. My brother has already gone to the State school for circus performers. So you see – we are very busy, and we know almost every town and every road and almost every village in Hungary, and they all know us.

But enough about us. I must tell you about Peep and the wild horse you call Tachi.

It happened this way. Our fair arrived one day in the village of Szil, but some weeks before our arrival the people there had captured a wild and shaggy and pretty little pony, the kind of pony most people in Szil had never seen before. And because nobody for 50 kilometres around knew anything about it, or whose it was, they decided it must belong to us. We were the only people they knew of who had ponies (which is what we use for giving children rides on).

The villagers had kept the pony behind a high wall at the back of the local factory where they make fruit boxes, but when they showed the pony to my father he had to tell them it was not ours. And that began a big discussion in the village about what to do with it. Though there were many different opinions, the majority and the mayor decided that we should have it anyway – if we wanted it.

'Horses need friends like everybody else,' the mayor said, 'and this pretty little horse needs to be among other small horses. Not among our big-boned old farm horses. Anyway, nobody is more likely to find the true owners in their travels than the Kosuth family. In the meantime, think of the children all over Hungary who will enjoy riding this pretty little mare.'

So the pony was given to my family, and as you have probably guessed it was your Shetland pony, Peep. The mayor had warned us that she was wild and difficult to approach. She would not even allow anyone to put a rope around her neck. My father said she would obviously need a lot of training and discipline before being trusted with children on her back. But our family have trained performing horses for generations so we did not think it would be a problem.

But it proved to be more difficult than we thought. Peep resisted everybody. She kicked and fought anybody who tried to get a rope over her neck. She was so wild that everybody thought she must have escaped from an untamed herd. But my father said, 'No. This pony has been tame one time or another. Tamed horses always look at you in a certain way, and this one has that look.'

I was not allowed into the yard with her, but one day when everybody was busy with the fair I was watching her through the wooden gate and she came right up to me and nudged me with her nose, just like a pet. Just like our own two riding ponies. She allowed me to pet her and rub her ears, and she obviously did not want me to go away.

I was so excited that I ran all the way to the square in front of the church where our fair was, and told my father. When he had finished putting up our tent he came with me to the yard and stood some distance away and told me to stand near the gate. When I did so the pony came up to me and tried to push her nose through the wooden bars of the tall gate.

'Open the gate and go in, Kato,' my father called.

I did so and the pony came up and nuzzled me and followed me around when I walked back and forth in the yard.

'She must have belonged to a girl like you,' Father said, and came over to the gate. But when my father came inside the yard, the pony began to back away again and swing her head back and forth very angrily.

That was how it all began. I became the only person who could approach her. Though you called her Peep, I named her 'Kudu' which means sugar in Magyar, but I will call her 'Peep' here for your sake.

Peep allowed me to do anything with her, even put a rope around her neck, and a little saddle on her back, although I did not try to ride her. But we could not get her to go near the other horses, or get her into the little field which the villagers loaned us for our horses. She simply refused to mix, and she kicked and bit and ran away when we tried to persuade her. My father, who knows so much about horses, said there must be a reason.

'She has got a mate or a foal somewhere nearby,' he said, 'and she is afraid that we will put her in a herd and take her away. She obviously does not want to desert the other horse.'

So next morning, before anyone was up and when the mist was still on the hard and frosty ground, my father and brother took Peep out of the yard and turned her loose in the street. Peep did not know what to do at first. But then she started to canter down the road, and my father and brother followed on our two ponies. About half an hour later Peep finally came to a little wood where there was a tall railway bridge over a valley. Peep stood under the bridge and whinnied, and then she walked about expectantly, until my father and brother suddenly saw another horse appear from nowhere. In fact he came out of the deep arches of the railway bridge, where he had obviously been hiding.

To cut a long story short, this horse was so sick and so weak that he could hardly move. And my father had never seen a horse like him. He thought at first he was a little mule, or a wild ass. But when he got a closer look he knew it was a true horse, and a very sick and wounded horse. There was plenty of grass in the area, but this horse was very thin and worn. It could hardly stand.

My father sent my brother back to fetch me, and I returned in one of our trucks with a rope. Peep was standing still, but she was not trying to get too close to this other horse, whom I know now is Tachi.

'I want you to lead Peep away,' my father said. 'And perhaps this one will follow her.'

'All right,' I said.

'I have never seen a horse quite like this one, Kato,' my father warned me. 'So be careful, because I think he is wild.'

He told me to put a rope over Peep, and that is what I did. Peep did not object, but when I began to lead her away she kept turning around to see that the other one was following. But whenever the wild horse stopped, Peep stopped. And like that, little by little, we got them onto the road, and we walked them very slowly to the village. Just outside the village, however, the wild horse lay down – too weak to go on. So Peep went back and stood near him.

We spent two more days in the village, and the wild horse could not get up from where he was lying. Finally my father brought all the other horses out near him and simply made them stand around him. They did not like it at all. My father said that they knew he was a wild horse. But at least they did not run away, and finally the wild horse got up on his legs and stood among them, almost as if he knew that he would die if he did not get up and move with them.

It was only when we finally got a good look at him that we saw how badly wounded he was. All his chest and front legs and neck were terribly cut, and the hard blood on the deep cuts was covered with flies. His right shoulder had bled all down his side, and his back legs were so badly cut that you could see the bones of his knees. It was terrible.

'It is a miracle he is till alive,' my father said. 'He must be a very tough little horse.'

We got him into our village enclosure by driving all the horses there together. Once he was inside the little village field, the wild horse collapsed again. By now everybody in the village wanted to see this extraordinary-looking horse, and I heard some people say it would be better to shoot him and end his misery. But I was very angry when I heard them say that. I rushed off to my father and begged him not to let them shoot the wild horse, and my father said not to worry.

'We will not let anyone shoot him. And anyway,' he said, 'when he is better he will be good for the fair. Look at the way the people rushed to see this strange little horse.'

But what could we do with him in the meantime? Nobody could get near the wild horse, even though he was lying down. If you got near him he would try to get up and kick and bite, and Peep would also get nervous and start kicking and biting at everybody – except me. So they thought I had better try to approach the wild horse first. However it was not so easy, because I could not help feeling nervous about it. He was such a strange animal. But I got up my courage and approached the two of them very carefully, while my father and brother stood nearby with big prod sticks, in case something happened. Fortunately Peep kept making little snorting noises of encouragement, and when I reached the wild horse he did not try to get up and bite me.

That was when I saw the dart hanging from his shoulder.

'He has got a little steel arrow in his shoulder,' I shouted out to my father. I did not know then what it was.

'See if you can pull it out, but be careful,' my father said. 'No, wait! I will get some cord.'

He got a ball of cord from the lorry and rolled it over to me. He told me to tie it to the dart and then he would pull it out while I stood clear.

The wild horse looked around at me with such a wild eye, such an angry and hurt but helpless and fierce look, that I

almost wept. I knew he must be in terrible pain. So I kept talking to him, and even Peep kept snorting encouragingly. So I did manage to tie the cord to the dart.

'Now come back,' my father called.

I got out of the way, and after they had carefully tightened the cord, my father gave it a tremendous jerk. It made the wild horse scream with pain, but the dart came out clean. It was an awful-looking thing, with little barbs on it like a fish hook. We wondered who had shot him with such a terrible thing in the first place. And why?

But it was impossible to sponge or tend the awful scars and wounds. My father would not let me risk touching the wild horse, although I wanted to. (I must tell you Kitty, that I want to become a nurse, but I do not think it will be possible, because I am probably not clever enough. Anyway we are never in one place long enough for me to do all the right things. I weep to myself some nights when I go to bed and think about it, because I long to study in the big hospital we always pass twice a year near the town of Cegled. There I would be able to see my parents and the fair whenever they came by. But I do not think I will be able to do it, because fair people are not important enough, although my teacher disagrees when I say this.)

Though we had taken the dart out of the wild horse's shoulder, he did not get better straight away, and we had a difficult time with him, because he slowed us down. But my father was determined to see that he got better. In fact we knew that the wild horse would stay quiet as long as Peep was with him. So we began our usual winter journey with both of them in our little herd. We were going east and south, and now that we have spoken to your grandfather we know that the wild horse probably stayed with us because we were going in the right direction for him. I suppose if we had gone north or west he would have left us, no matter how weak or sick he was. And taken Peep with him.

Anyway, Kitty, I eventually trained Peep to carry children, and she did it very well and gladly, although she would still not allow anybody else but me to groom her. Meanwhile, the wild horse stayed quietly with the others, slowly recuperating. And though he was frantic the first time we took Peep away for her training, he calmed down when he realized that we always brought her back. But nobody *ever* managed to touch the wild horse, or get near to him. Not even me. Whenever he was in a village field with the other horses he would always stand alone, or rather lie down alone, because it was a long time before he was able to stand up properly. Your grandfather eventually told us that, apart from his wounds, the drugged dart had probably been pumping poison slowly into his blood stream, because it had not gone in deep enough in the first place.

But as we travelled on, the wild horse got better and better, and he soon began to be more and more restless, spending all his time simply walking around and around any enclosure we put him into. Your grandfather asked us how we crossed the Danube without being stopped by the people who were watching out for Tachi and Peep on the bridges. It was very simple. There is a ferry, a sort of floating bridge pulled by diesel motors, near the village Paks. We have always used it because it is on our usual route. But there was no one watching there for the two horses, because they never expected a wild horse to use such a thing.

In fact we had just crossed the river and had set up the fair in the village Dunapartaj, when we noticed that the wild horse was no longer in the enclosure with the other horses. He had knocked some palings out of a shed and escaped. We hunted everywhere for him, but could not find him. We spent four days in Dunapartaj, and even delayed our departure for a day, but eventually we had to leave without him, which made us very sad. But what else could we do?

But the next day as we moved along the main road to Kishoks I looked out of the back of our caravan and saw the wild horse following us along the edge of the road in the snow. We tried to catch him again, but he was too clever for us. And thereafter he simply followed us at a safe distance, and we let him do it without bothering him.

'No point in chasing him,' my father said. 'As long as we have his little mate he will follow us.'

Tachi went on following us wherever we went. He always hid himself outside the villages when we stopped for a few days. Once, a whole week passed in a village and we did not see him. But he always appeared again when we left. This went on right across eastern Hungary until we reached the Ukrainian border, the furthermost point east in our country. It is always there that we turn around to go back west again.

The first night after we turned back westwards, we stopped our fair in the village of Negrded, which is famous for its cherry orchards. We were given one of the little orchards to turn our horses loose in, and by now we had obviously grown careless about Peep.

The result? We could not find her one morning when we came to get her. We searched the cherry orchard which was deep in snow, and finally we found tracks that led to a deep canal at one end of the orchard. We had been sure that the horses would never cross it, because it was very deep and it was not frozen over. But that morning we found that there was one little corner of it that *was* frozen over, and we saw two lots of tracks on the snow. Obviously Tachi had come into the orchard, across the ice, to get Peep and take her away.

We searched the fields, the woods and the other orchards, but they had gone, and though all the villagers helped us, we decided after four days that it was hopeless.

We never saw Peep or the wild horse again. They had just disappeared into our white Hungarian snow, and we did not realize how fond we had become of *both* of them until they had gone for ever. I think I loved little Peep as much as you did, Kitty, even though she was only with us a short time. I must have wept for her as much as you did. But the trouble is that I never knew who Peep really was, or who she belonged to, or where she and Tachi came from. So they had gone the way they had come – from nowhere.

It was weeks later, when one of our horses needed the attention of a veterinary in the town of Miskolc, that my father told the vet about the two strange horses. The vet immediately became excited and telephoned Budapest. Four days later your grandfather came all the way from London to see us, and we learned then the true history of Peep and Tachi – the wild horse.

Your grandfather spent a whole evening telling us all about the two horses and about you, Kitty. Your grandfather asked me to write down everything that had happened, which I have done in Magyar, with the help of our teacher, Miss Nagy. I suppose I have left out quite a lot, but I think I have put down everything important.

Knowing now that the wild horse is heading for his home in Mongolia, we think that he and Peep must have already crossed the Carpathian mountains (cold and frozen) and will be somewhere in the Ukraine steppes which must also be cold and frozen.

Please let me know when you or your Mongolian friend have any news of them. Your grandfather has promised to write to my father if he has any news. The wild horse looked so ugly and sick when we first saw him that it was difficult to like him, although we all felt sorry for him. But as soon as he began to get better everybody in our family became fascinated with him, and admired him very much, because I think we all guessed he had something on his mind all the time – some purpose which made everything else unimportant.

It would be nice if you would write to me in any case.

Write in English. We will find someone to translate it for us. Many people in our villages have lived in America, Australia or Canada, or even in England. One man in the village of Gyoma lived for ten years in a strange country called the Isle of Man where the cats have no tails. Do you know it? He is a baker.

Greetings, dear friend of Peep and Tachi, dear friend to all wild animals.

(Signed)
Kato Kosuth

PS I have written all the addresses where you can write to me on a separate piece of paper, so please pin it inside the big box you keep your clothes in, which is where I always keep important things I do not want to lose. K.K.

And that, Baryut, is the sad letter from Kato Kosuth. But if Tachi and Peep are now in the Ukraine they are getting nearer to you than they are to me, so please try to find out what you can about them. In fact you will probably know more than I do from here on.

Nothing more to add, absolutely nothing, because I don't see how they'll ever cross those vast, white, frozen steppes and the huge rivers that flow in the Ukraine. It looks like half the world on the map. Grandfather has written to two professors in Kiev, the capital of the Ukraine, so we hope that somebody there will be looking after them. K.

14

Dear Kitty,

When our friend Gritti read your last letter (he reads English now) he was sitting on a lorry, and the moment he had finished it he leapt off and said, 'She is absolutely right, Baryut. They are almost half-way home! Do you realize that?'

He was so excited that he immediately rushed off to get in touch with his professor in Ulan Bator to ask him if he knew that Tachi and Peep were now in the Ukraine. The professor said of course he knew. Your grandfather had already sent him a telegram. In fact the professor in Ulan Bator has already promised him that they would do everything possible to find Tachi and Peep before they had gone very far.

But I am not too optimistic, Kitty. In Mongolian we say, 'Do not tell your fortune until it has happened.' That is the same as your English expression 'Do not count your chickens before they are hatched.' I learned that myself. My aunt says I am a good pupil in English, but have a bad memory. Anyway, we will just have to wait now.

Gritti wanted to fly off to the Ukraine and look for Tachi and Peep himself. But that was not practicable. Where would he begin?

And how, after reading Kato Kosuth's letter, I am still hoping that Peep and Tachi will be captured, even though they are getting nearer home. Too many terrible things seem to be happening to them, so I prefer them to be caught rather than risk any more injuries or terrible experiences.

I will write the moment we hear anything more. Meanwhile, much love to you all.

Your sincere friend,
Baryut

15

Dear Kitty,

News at last!

But I do not know what to think. I suppose everything that happened this time was inevitable. But I wish we lived in neighbouring villages. Then I could ride over and ask you what you think about it.

The first word anyone had in Kiev (capital of Ukraine) of Tachi and Peep came from a signal woman on one of the Ukrainian railway lines. One night, on a hilly and difficult part of the line near the village of Lipovetz, a signal woman was standing in the blinding snow holding up her yellow flag while a train went by (that is what all signal people have to do there), when she saw by the light of the carriages two very small and very unusual-looking horses galloping wildly along the railway line.

She reported it to the station-master at Uman, because stray animals are a danger to trains. Fortunately the train driver had also seen them, and he too reported it. But it was only weeks later that these reports were read in Kiev, where someone realized what the two unusual-looking horses were. By which time Tachi and Peep were lost again.

Then they were seen on a collective farm in the district of Cherkassy. They had sheltered from a snow storm for two or three nights behind a village repair shop. Tachi had kicked down the door of a silo, and they had eaten some oats and corn and then disappeared. The next report came from a goose farm, part of the collective farm of Gradisk, where two women who looked after a thousand white geese were frightened one day by two little horses who just rose up suddenly like birds in a field and galloped through the flock of geese, scattering them right and left. (What a sight that must have been.)

These reports were not very important, but they did give the Ukrainian professors an idea of where the horses were. So the Ukrainian Academy of Sciences sent a special professor named Nemchenko to try to organize their capture. They also sent for Gritti, who flew to Ulan Bator and then to Kiev and then to Kharkov in the Ukraine, where he met Professor Nemchenko.

At first Gritti and Nemchenko (who is also a zoologist) tried to track down the two horses, but they found it impossible because the spring snows were beginning to melt, and the Ukrainian steppes were already so thick with black mud that you could not move anywhere but on the main roads. They had no hope of getting across the muddy fields. A tractor could have done it, but the tractors were all busy with spring ploughing and sowing, so they could not be spared. It was therefore impossible to look in the likely places where Tachi and Peep would be.

'There is only one way to do this,' Professor Nemchenko said. 'We will ask the Red Army to help us.'

'How?' Gritti asked him. 'What can they do?'

'I do not know,' Nemchenko said. 'But they have helicopters. And after all, is it not the Army's job to be able to cross muddy steppes and swollen rivers without bothering about roads and bridges and mud?'

And that was how the Red Army chase started, with two Red Army units setting out after Tachi and Peep who simply kept going on and on, night and day. It took the army a week to pick up their tracks, and finally the two horses were spotted by an army helicopter lying in a little clump of thin birch trees on the muddy bank of a flooded river. In fact it was so muddy and flooded that it was hopeless for jeeps or trucks to try to get there. So the Red Army commander decided to send two amphibious tanks to help. They could get through anything.

Gritti went in one tank, and Professor Nemchenko went in the other. And what they hoped to do was to trap the horses in a big bend of the river, so that their path ahead and on each side would be blocked by water, and the two tanks would then block their retreat from behind.

The army tanks arrived at the place after dark, and they could find no trace of Tachi and Peep. But they guessed that the two horses were still trying to cross the river, so the tanks split up. One went along the river bank downstream, the other went upstream. They both had powerful searchlights, and they could travel much faster than a horse. They also hoped that the terrible noise of the tanks would frighten Tachi and keep him moving, and therefore visible to them.

The tank that Gritti was in shone its searchlight all along the river bank while Gritti sat up in the opening of the tank with field glasses. But apart from frightening birds and rabbits he saw nothing for about two hours. Then suddenly there was a beige flash in the searchlight and Gritti knew he had found them.

'Hold still,' he shouted to the tank commander.

The tank stopped, and Gritti shouted to the soldier operating the searchlight to keep it on the fleeing figure of the horse. It was certainly Tachi. But where was Peep?

At first Gritti thought that Tachi was just running away in a panic. But in fact Tachi was running around in a large circle. They kept the light on him until they saw that Peep was in the middle of Tachi's circle. She was stuck up to her belly in a big, black mud hole and could not move. Tachi was circling around her, throwing up mud with his galloping hoofs, and he was either trying to divert attention from her, or he was preparing to attack the tanks to protect her.

In any case Peep was stuck fast, and Tachi was obviously not going to leave her.

'We have got them,' Gritti shouted excitedly over the radio to Professor Nemchenko in the other tank.

While they waited for the other tank to arrive, Gritti's tank tried to get nearer to Peep. But every time they approached her, Tachi swung around and came straight for the tank in one of his aggressive attacks.

'Stop the tank,' Gritti shouted to the commander.

'What for?' the commander said.

'He'll attack us,' Gritti shouted.

The commander laughed. He was not going to believe that a horse would attack a tank. 'Do not worry,' he said. 'He will not bother us.'

But Gritti was shouting, 'Turn around! Get out of the way! He will attack us and he will kill himself! Turn around!'

The commander could see that Gritti meant it, and that Tachi also meant it, so he gave the order, and the tank swung around quickly and fled from Tachi, who galloped furiously after it. Only when they were quite clear did they stop the tank and turn out the searchlight and listen. They could hear Tachi snorting and screaming in fury.

'We will wait here until it is light,' Gritti told the commander, heaving a very big sigh of relief.

'That crazy horse!' the commander said incredulously. 'What is he trying to do?' But then he had to laugh at the idea of a horse making his tank flee.

The tank stayed there all night, only turning on its searchlight every now and then to make sure that Peep was all right and not too deep in the mud. She was still struggling to get out, but Gritti knew enough about horses now to know that Peep would probably wait patiently for daylight before trying to get out. Unless Tachi tried to hurry her up.

The other tank was now near enough to wait with them, and just before it began to be light, Tachi, who had been restless all night, began to encourage Peep to get out.

By now all the soldiers knew about Tachi and Peep's long journey, and they were anxious to help. But they knew that they would have to capture Tachi and get him out of the way before they could help Peep, or even get near her. At first they wanted to get out of their tanks and creep up on Tachi with ropes and try to catch him. But Gritti told them that Tachi was too clever and even too dangerous to let them do that. In fact it would only be possible if they could get more help from collective farmers. If there were enough of them they might be able to surround Tachi. But when it began to be light, Gritti realized that the country was far too open to catch Tachi that way either.

So Gritti decided to call in the special army helicopters fitted with rocket nets. There was nothing else he could do.

'Rocket nets' are something the army helicopters carry to lay a net path across mud, or to put a net cover over anything that needs quick camouflage, or simply something that needs to be climbed up, such as a bombed-out building or steep river banks. The nets are fired by rockets from under the helicopter, and the tank commander was sure that if one of these nets was dropped on Tachi he would never escape.

At eight o'clock the army helicopter appeared in the sky, and Gritti used the tank's radio to explain to the pilot what the situation was.

'When you drop your net,' Gritti told him on the radio, 'please be sure that you drop it so that the horse is right in the middle of it, and is completely covered. If you only half-cover him he will escape. And he has already had such a bad experience with a barbed-wire fence that we do not want that sort of thing to happen again.'

'Don't worry,' the pilot said. 'We could stop an elephant.'

At first the helicopter just hovered over the two horses, which only made Tachi frantic. He began whinnying and stamping his feet, and once he even charged Peep, as if telling her to try harder. But poor little Peep only seemed to sink deeper into the mud. She was whinnying pathetically because she obviously knew now that she was never going to get out by herself. Tachi seemed to know it too, and he was almost out of his mind.

When the helicopter came in low and hovered closer and closer, with its huge blades whipping up the water and the black mud, Tachi began to run around madly in small circles, waving his head furiously, and finally standing on his fore legs and kicking up at the helicopter.

Meanwhile Gritti was telling the pilot on the radio to be careful, for heaven sake! But to be quick! He had never seen a net fired from a helicopter, so he was amazed when there was a sudden explosion and four rockets went off and a huge square nylon net spread out and was driven down to earth.

'Bull's eye!' the pilot shouted on the radio.

The net had fallen on Tachi like a huge hand, wrapping itself around him and bringing him down on his knees, and then on his side. He was screaming in fury and kicking his legs wildly and snapping his teeth. But he was caught like a fish, and the more he struggled the more entangled he became.

But something else had also happened.

The net had not only covered Tachi, but a corner of it had also fallen on Peep. And because there was a lot of force behind it, and because the net itself was very heavy, Peep was driven deeper into the mud. In fact it was quite clear that she was about to go right under.

'Hurry!' Gritti shouted at his tank commander now. 'Get close to her!'

The tank's engine was cold and it took time to start. In the meantime the helicopter hovered over the spot, and the pilot shouted to them over the radio that they had better hurry. He said he would try to lift the net off Peep, and they dropped a special hook which was used for recovering the net, and that way they managed to lift the corner of the net clear of Peep.

The two tanks were as close as they could get to Peep now, and because the soldiers were all so keen, they had already unloaded all the canvas turret covers which they threw onto the mud. Then one soldier crawled over the sagging canvas to Peep and shouted back that she was breathing with great difficulty. The mud was obviously pressing heavily on her chest, and she was drowning in it.

'I do not think she is going to last long,' the soldier said.

Gritti was now almost as frantic as Tachi, because all your letters, Kitty, had made Peep so close to all of us that she was terribly important to him too.

Gritti said he kept thinking to himself, 'What has she done, this pretty little English mare, to deserve this? What is she doing out here, so far away from home, drowning in the Ukrainian mud?'

By now Gritti could see that the mud hole was really an old water pond. A huge slide of black earth, soaked by the spring thaw, had slipped into it and turned it into a pool of mud, which meant that it was much deeper than Peep's legs. She would obviously disappear very soon if she was not pulled out quick.

The soldier crawled back to the tank. 'The only way you will get her out is to pull her straight up,' he told them. 'She will never be able to move forward, no matter what you do.'

'In that case,' Gritti said, because he was really in charge of the operation, 'the helicopter can put a harness on me and I will crawl out and try to get one of these canvas sheets under her belly so that the helicopter can lift her out.'

It was a risky business, but the helicopter lowered a steel cable with a harness on it, and Gritti put it on. Held up by the helicopter, he crawled out to Peep. He had one of the tank engine covers with him, and he pushed it down into the mud near Peep with his feet. When he began to sink too deep into the mud, he signalled the helicopter to tighten the cable that held him.

'Pull me out,' he shouted.

They winched him up, and he got to the other side of Peep and again went down feet first into the mud. But this time he had to put his head and arms under the mud and simply disappear so that he could get the canvas sheet under Peep's stomach.

It was a brave thing to do – disappearing into that mud. What if the cable holding him had broken? Or if he got stuck under Peep? After all, it was not water but thick gluey jelly with no bottom to it. The pilot waited for a while, and then the tank commander told him to winch Gritti up. When his muddy head and shoulders appeared, Gritti was holding the canvas. He had managed to get it under Peep's stomach.

The helicopter lifted Peep out, and she hung in the air under the helicopter. She seemed all right. But Gritti knew she would gallop off the moment she was free, so he tied her feet together while she was still suspended in mid-air. Then they let her down again.

Now they had to think about Tachi. He was still struggling in the net. But Gritti and the soldiers managed to tie his legs before the helicopter hooked the net away, which left Tachi and Peep lying trussed like chickens to await their fate.

By now it was afternoon, and when the helicopter landed nearby, all the soldiers and fliers and Gritti and Professor Nemchenko ate their lunch, while one of the soldiers washed some of the mud off poor Peep. When they had finished lunch they lifted the two horses into the helicopter, and with Gritti and Nemchenko aboard, it flew off to the nearest Red Army headquarters, where Peep and Tachi were put into a high-walled enclosure usually reserved for guns and tanks.

That is where they are now, Kitty. It is 400 kilometres east of where they were actually caught. Gritti says that Tachi has terrible scars all over him, not only on his chest but even under his stomach, rump and head. Half his tail has been pulled out. There is still an open, festering wound where the dart hit him on the shoulder. Peep, on the other hand, was not injured anywhere, but she was thin and weak, and her hoofs were badly worn and chipped. A large part of her tail had also been pulled out, as if it had been caught in something. Peep would not eat the bran and oats they gave her, but would only eat hay.

Of course the moment Tachi was released in the army tank enclosure he began to stamp around, looking for a way out. But

Gritti says there is no way out of that enclosure. In any case they will both be kept there for some time. Then they will be taken to the State Quarantine farm at Nikolskaya, which is another 300 kilometres to the east. There they will be tested to see if they have brought in any animal diseases, and they will probably have to stay there in quarantine for weeks and weeks.

That is the situation now, Kitty. This letter has taken Gritti and me a whole week to write, and of course it is really what Gritti has been telling me. But soon you will have Peep and Tachi back again, so please let me know the moment they arrive. And please report everything they do, and what you think of them. I mean their appearance and their character. Tell me exactly what Peep does when she sees you for the first time.

With sad and happy greetings,
I remain, your friend,
Baryut

PS Gritti says Peep is a very very pretty little pony. He says he told the army how clever and determined Tachi is, and to be careful. They said they understood. But Gritti thinks they underestimate Tachi, like everybody who does not really know him. He also thinks that Tachi, being a wild horse, knows how near home he is, and he will now be more desperate than ever to get free again. Gritti thinks he will use every trick he knows. So we wait nervously until the day when your grandfather comes to collect them from the State farm and finally takes them back again to the safety of your Reserve in Wales. B.

16

Dear Baryut,

Mrs Evans actually cried and said, 'It just goes to show', when I read your letter aloud. Grandfather just groaned, and all I could do was heave a sigh of relief, because I don't think Peep could have lasted much longer if they had kept going.

But now we are getting everything ready for them. Grandfather has had all the fences strengthened and raised by three feet. The stone walls have been checked and cemented, and all bridges and exits have been double gated.

You remember Peter in the Crow's Nest? He now has three more look-out posts, which means that he can see into all the valleys and the woods. (We now have some red deer.)

So all we can do now is to wait excitedly for the return of our exiles.

But I'm also excited about something else. My own father is coming home next month. Not for good, but for six weeks. He'll be coming back home for good next year. I don't suppose he'll recognize me. In fact he won't really know me at all, will he? That's why I'm feeling a bit nervous. I don't even know what to think or hope for. I could never leave Grandfather and Mrs Evans! I wish you *did* live in the next village, Baryut, then we could meet half-way to discuss everything. I have plenty of friends at school, but I don't seem to be able to talk to them seriously. I'm sure I could explain everything to you, although what language do you think we could use? I gave up trying to learn Mongolian, so it would have to be something like Monglish or Engolian.

This seems to be mostly about myself, so I shall put an end to it before I start feeling depressed. Life gets more and more complicated, doesn't it? I used to think it would get more and more simple.

I'll let you know the moment I hear anything about Peep and Tachi.

Love to you all,
Kitty

17

Dear Kitty,

More trouble! Nothing ever seems to go right. I wonder why.

I do not know what it is, but Gritti has been sent for again. He left for the Ukraine yesterday. Something is wrong. They would not tell Gritti anything. They just told him to get back to the State farm as quickly as possible.

Gritti did not want to leave here, because the wild herd has been trying desperately to break out of the mountains lately. They obviously know now that they are locked in. Our scientists have spent a lot of time sealing off many of their escape routes by making landslides, or by simply building walls. Also, the old master stallion finally died, and the young one who has taken his place is not very intelligent. He seems to keep the herd rushing here and there and everywhere at the gallop, but without any sense. The foals and the old mares cannot keep up, so the herd is in danger of splitting up. Or of exhausting themselves just before winter, which means that many will probably die when it gets cold.

That is why Gritti is very worried about them. That is why he secretly wishes Tachi was back. Tachi would not have been so stupid.

That is all I have to tell you at the moment, Kitty, until I hear from Gritti.

Until then, I still remain,
Your ever-loving friend,
Baryut

18

Dear Kitty,

Well, I did not like to say anything, but I knew that the more they put Tachi in and out of horse-vans and enclosures, or moved him from one place to the other, the more chances he would have of breaking free.

It happened when they were being shifted from an airfield to the State Quarantine farm at Nikolskaya, just across the Volga. The army had flown them to the nearest airfield in a big transport plane, because it was too far away for a helicopter. The State farm sent a horse-van to pick them up, and though the driver and the attendant had been warned about Tachi's tricks, they did not realise how clever he was. So when they put him into the horse-van, which was enclosed, they actually untied his legs, thinking he was safe once he was in the van.

But after they had travelled about 30 kilometres Tachi began to kick the side of the van. And he went on kicking until they decided they had better stop and take a look.

The one thing they had been warned not to do was to get into the van with Tachi. But the attendant thought he would just open the back gate of the horse-van – just open it a crack – and take a quick look. That is all he did, Gritti said. He just opened it a crack. The next moment Tachi had kicked the door down, knocking the attendant unconscious. Of course he leapt out instantly. He stood for a moment snorting and waiting for Peep to follow him. Then he put his head down and charged the driver who had come to help his wounded comrade. When the driver had also been knocked down Tachi and Peep galloped off across the fields which were planted with maize. They disappeared completely into it, and nothing more was seen of Tachi and Peep.

The chairman of the State Quarantine farm did his best to organize a search, but they finally had to send to Mongolia for Gritti. They hoped Gritti could advise them on the behaviour of the wild horse, because they had not been able to find any trace of either horse. All Gritti could do was to tell them how Tachi would hide by day and move by night, and that he would go on moving east, always east, always heading for home.

That was three months ago.

Since then they have searched every corner of the country east of Nikolskaya, every possible hiding place. They have warned all the collective farms, the villages, the railway stations, and asked the army for their help. They have been over the fields in trucks and jeeps and helicopters and on horseback. And the telephone lines have been burning up, because everybody is angry with everybody else. But they have not found any sign of Tachi and Peep.

That is the story so far, Kitty. The country they are in now is very flat and open, but with fewer and fewer villages. But soon, if they keep going east, they will be in the great open steppes and desert of Kazakhstan, and perhaps in the mountains of Kirghizia, and I do not think they will ever be captured there. It is very wild country. In fact it is also horse country, although there is not a lot of feed in those bare, snowy mountains.

But this time, Kitty, I do hope that Tachi reaches our mountains. I hope they are not caught. I cannot help feeling it this time.

In any case I will not be in our mountain pastures much

longer. I will leave here next September to go to Kobdo, where I will finish my ten-year schooling. Do you realize that we have been writing to each other for almost two years? I cannot believe it. Everything seems like yesterday's sunrise.

With warmest greetings and salutations,
I remain,
Your old friend,
Baryut

PS What has happened to your dog Skip? You never write about him any more. I hope he is all right. My dog (named Khan) was killed last May when he was chasing quail in our grasslands. He was a happy little dog, always laughing and digging holes and wagging his tail, and even when he was dying he tried to wag his tail, as if he was telling us not to be upset, although his eyes were very sad. He was killed because he ran in front of a tractor, which was raking up cut grass. In our district we do not like to bury dogs. We say they should be buried by the sun. In other words not buried at all. But my sister Miza and I were determined to bury him, so we crept out one night and rode into the mountains and buried Khan the way our ancestors used to bury their favourite horses – as their best friends. Poor little Khan. He was so happy that I often used to wonder what it would be like to be a dog, to be that gay and happy all the time. B.

19

Dear Baryut,

No word from you for four and a half months.

What's happening? Are you waiting for news? Or is the news so bad that you don't want to tell me? Grandfather was furious with everybody when he read your last letter. He knew they were going to underestimate Tachi's cunning and determination.

Please write when you have even the slightest piece of news. Anything.

Yours ever,
Kitty

* * * * *

Dear Kitty,

I have been busy, studying for my physics and chemistry tests, and Aunt Seroghli was away visiting the Foreign Languages Institute in Sverdlovsk. That is why I have not written before.

Gritti came back home after four months searching for them in planes, helicopters, cars, trucks, tractors and on horse and foot. He thinks that they are now dead somewhere in Kazakhtan – probably of exhaustion, or because they ate poisoned roots they did not know about, or drank naturally-poisoned water. Or they could have died for lack of water or lack of food. He says a hundred things could have killed them on those wild Kazakh steppes. They are full of trouble.

And there is really no other news.

That is all I can say at the moment.

Your friend,
Baryut

* * * * *

Dear Baryut,

This is a postcard of Tower Bridge in London. I am spending four days in London with someone who may become my stepmother soon. I read in the papers yesterday that Mongolia and China are having a really terrible winter. It's now six months since Tachi and Peep disappeared, and I suppose you've definitely given up all hope now. I still can't believe it, though. Love, Kitty

*   *   *   *   *

Dear Kitty,

I am writing this postcard myself. This English is by myself, with the help of my teacher. This card is a picture of our Mongolian hero, Suhe-Bator. I have now left our mountains. I am studying at school No. 4 in the town of Kobdo. Our winter has been the coldest in history, with 30 degrees of frost. Many horses in our district died, including some of the wild herd. Tachi and Peep have now disappeared for ever, which is very sad. It is now 9 months after they disappeared. They must have died in the terrible cold. Goodbye, Kitty. Baryut

*   *   *   *   *

Dear Baryut,

Just a card to say I can't help thinking of Peep and Tachi even though they've gone for good. I still drop a tear for them. I keep imagining them huddled up somewhere in the cold snow, or freezing to death in those bare, windy mountains. I now have a new stepmother who is very nice. Soon I will leave the Reserve for good, worse luck, and go to Portsmouth to live. Mrs Evans is very upset. As for Grandfather!! That's about all this card will take. Your English is fabulous. I am just beginning my exams. Very hard and very grindy (difficult). Love, Kitty

*　　*　　*　　*　　*

Dear Kitty,

Our Academy of Sciences at Ulan Bator has received a report that two wild horses have been seen by a geologist 100 kilometres to the west of our mountains. Gritti wrote to me and said it might be Tachi and Peep. But I doubt it. I think it is probably two of the five wild horses which were always missing from the herd. Remember? I counted 31 and there were only 26. I think that is what they are.

In any case I will write the moment I have found out anything at all.

Yours sincerely,
Baryut

*　　*　　*　　*　　*

Dear Baryut,

If it *is* them, please send me a telegram. Even so, I don't really believe it either. But I can't help feeling excited and hopeful again. Grandfather says you can send the telegram 'collect' (paid here) if you like.

Your expectant and rather breathless friend,
Kitty

*　　*　　*　　*　　*

ULAN BATOR. ELT. MISS KITTY JAMIESON WILDLIFE RESERVE BLACK MOUNTAINS WALES.
DEAR FRIEND. TACHI AND PEEP HAVE DEFINITELY APPEARED IN

OUR MOUNTAINS BUT HAVE NOT YET BEEN FOUND. WILL WRITE YOU FULL DETAILS WHEN EVERYTHING IS CLEAR. YOUR EXCITED FRIEND BARYUT.

20

Dear Kitty,

It is the usual incredible story, as everything is with Tachi and Peep. In fact part of it is almost too difficult and painful to write, but it must be written.

It was on the 5th of March that another geologist, who was working in our mountains, reported on his radio to his headquarters that he had seen two wild horses walking through one of the long valleys of our mountains with great difficulty.

When the news spread (I was home on holiday) everyone wanted to hurry off immediately to the long valley to see if we could find the two wild horses. My brother, sister, father, uncles, and even my mother and grandfather wanted to go. And, of course, Aunt Seroghli. But we could not all go, so four of us went: my father, Gritti, Aunt Seroghli and myself.

We set out early one morning and by late afternoon we had reached the farthest point in our long valley; and just as we got there the wild herd also appeared. But they were all so nervous that they obviously knew something was happening. The young master stallion was prancing about as if he were a circus horse, and then suddenly he turned the whole herd away, and they galloped out of sight.

About ten minutes later Tachi and Peep appeared. I cannot tell you how I felt, Kitty. It was almost too much for all of us. I could see little silver tears in Aunt Seroghli's eyes. (It is quite true!)

'So that is the little English mare!' my father said again and again. 'So that is the faithful little mare!' he kept repeating.

We had all heard so much about Peep from you that we felt we knew her as well as we know our own horses. More so! We all thought of you, Kitty. Every one of us.

'But she is going to have a foal at any moment,' Gritti said then.

It was obvious to all of us, and Tachi simply stood near her and twitched his ears and waved his head as if he were helpless to do anything for her. She was very heavy, and she was moving very slowly, with great difficulty. It was painful to watch her. Finally she got down on her front knees and then lay down. Tachi nudged her once or twice, then he suddenly galloped across the valley, tossing his head and whinnying aggressively and stamping his feet. Finally he lifted his head and let out a snort that was almost a scream.

'He will have to fight the young stallion if he wants the whole herd now,' my father pointed out. 'And he knows it.'

'Perhaps he just wants Peep,' Aunt Seroghli said. 'Perhaps he will not mix with the others at all. Maybe they will stick together . . .'

'He will mix,' my father said. 'Look at him . . .'

Tachi was galloping around as if he were taking possession of the place, and he also seemed to be whipping up his temper. By the time we had to leave, Tachi had gone off to explore his homeland, while Peep simply stayed where she was, as if that was all that was left for her now – that and patience.

Of course everybody met us with a thousand questions, and finally we got out the big map and traced their journey across the world. And though everybody admired Tachi's fierce determination to reach home, we also thought how marvellous it was that your tame little English mare had made the incredible journey with him.

But then we began to argue about what should be done with them. Should Tachi be sent back to your Reserve in Wales? Or should Peep be sent back without him? And the foal? It

could not stay in the wild herd, because it was not going to be a pure wild horse. It would be half Peep. But I think we all knew that it did not really matter what we said. The whole question would be decided by the scientists.

It was my sister Miza who asked my father when he thought Peep's foal would be born.

My father has a black moustache, and when he starts rubbing it with the knuckle of his thumb we all know that something is wrong.

'Well?' my mother said to him.

'I think the little English horse will have her foal tomorrow or the next day,' he said. 'And we must be very careful not to disturb her. Very, very careful.'

We knew then that something was worrying him, but he refused to say anything more. I went back next day with my father and Gritti to see that Peep was all right, and when we crept up the side of the little hill overlooking the long valley, we saw that the whole herd was there. In the middle of the herd was the young master stallion, and he was confronting Tachi who stood near Peep.

'Now they will fight it out,' Gritti whispered.

The young master stallion stamped around and made a lot of fuss, as if he was telling the herd to start moving. They all obeyed him except Tachi and Peep. Peep was on her feet, but she looked as if she was too blown to move. Her head was down, and her whole manner was droopy and heavy. Tachi simply stood near her as if he was watching to see what the young stallion would do. In fact it was obviously going to be their first test of strength.

'It is now or never,' I said, watching Tachi.

The moment I said it, the young stallion suddenly charged at Peep from behind, as if he was telling her to get a move on. But Tachi stood in the way with his head down. And at the last moment Tachi turned quickly and kicked the young stallion so hard that he was almost knocked over. But he recovered, and he turned and tried to kick Tachi, who simply leapt out of the way and then charged the young stallion. Again he almost knocked the young stallion over, and it was all done with incredible speed.

'Amazing,' my father said. 'I have never seen a horse move so quickly.'

The stallion tried once more to force Peep to obey, but Peep stood painfully still, Tachi butted and kicked the stallion so fiercely that he screamed in pain. Normally this would have been the beginning of a real fight. But instead of going after the young stallion and following up his advantage, Tachi remained close to Peep and simply waved his head around. The young stallion made a lot of fuss about it, but he did not charge again. He snorted and puffed, and then he turned around and galloped off after the herd. Tachi did not try to chase him. In fact he did nothing at all.

'He knows the little mare is in trouble,' my father said.

'What sort of trouble?' I asked my father, knowing all the time that he was hiding something.

'I think Peep has injured her pelvic basin,' he said, 'and she is going to have serious trouble giving birth to her foal. That is why she is standing so still. It is probably very painful for her to move at all.'

'Can we not help?' Gritti asked.

'We dare not disturb her, or excite her,' my father said.

'But if we did it carefully . . .'

But my father shook his head. 'If we go down there to help her, Tachi will become frantic, and Peep will probably try to run away. That would be dangerous for her. We can only wait . . .'

So there was really nothing we could do for her. We watched her the whole day, and Peep simply stood there without moving, while Tachi kept running circles around her and nibbling at her mane and tail. That night we rode home feeling very worried and unhappy, because we had seen enough of Peep now to know how weak and worn out she was, and how forlorn she looked so far away from her little English hillsides.

Next morning we went back again to the long valley, but Peep and Tachi had gone. Tachi still knew these mountains better than we did, and though we searched everywhere very carefully we could not find them. We went on searching all that day and all the next day, but we still did not find them. The third morning we were just setting out from our tents when we heard a helicopter.

'I asked the Academy if they would send us one,' Gritti said. 'I thought if we flew over high enough we might find them without disturbing them.'

We waved to the helicopter, and when they saw us they landed in a little basin near us. We left our horses, and all three of us got aboard and off we went over the mountains. We flew very high and began to look into all the little valleys and tributaries, until at about 2 o'clock we saw some black dots way below us in a patch of dead saxifrage.

'It is them,' Gritti shouted above the clatter of the machine.

At first we could not see them clearly, but as the pilot took us right over them, we could see even from that great height that it was Tachi and Peep.

'And Peep has already given birth to her foal!' I shouted. I could see three dark dots.

'Go down a little lower,' my father called out to the pilot.

When we came down lower we could distinguish Peep lying down on some gravel and near her was the little new-born foal. Tachi was standing up. But as the helicopter came down over them he became frantic and began to gallop around and around Peep. The foal also tried to get to its feet, but it could not stand up.

Only Peep did not move, and I knew by the look of her, Kitty, that poor Peep was already dead.

'We are too late!' I shouted rather hysterically. 'She is dead.'

'Maybe she is too exhausted to get up,' Gritti said.

'No. She is dead,' my father said sadly.

I am sorry, Kitty, but it is no use telling you anything else. Peep was dead. We all knew it, and we also knew that we would have to rescue her little foal very quickly, otherwise it too would die. So my father told the pilot that we must go down and get it.

'If the helicopter gets too near them,' Gritti argued, 'Tachi will probably try to carry the foal away in his teeth.' He remembered the time when Tachi had actually carried a foal like that.

'We will have to chance that,' my father said.

He told the pilot to land as near as possible to the three horses, and when we came down about fifty metres from them, stirring up dust and dry little stones, Tachi was furious. He rushed at the machine, then back to the foal and Peep. When we got out of the helicopter he charged us, trying to kick us. We scattered. But we were waving coats, and then the pilot fired a Very pistol to frighten him off.

'Hurry,' I said, 'before he tries to take the foal.'

But when we moved towards Peep and the foal, Tachi stood over them again, and this time he lifted the foal in his teeth and literally threw it forward: once, twice, three times. He moved it about 50 metres.

We knew he would kill it if he kept doing that to it, and the nearer we got the more reckless he became. In fact we thought we would have to give up. But when we were about ten metres from the poor dead Peep, Tachi suddenly dropped the foal and rushed back to her and tried to lift her with his teeth, which gave us a chance to get the foal.

It was not much bigger than a large dog, and our big pilot snatched it off its four legs like a baby and ran back to the machine. He had not gone far when Tachi began to chase him, and I think Tachi would have killed the pilot if he had managed to catch him. But we went on waving our coats and shouting, and one of the crew fired a Very pistol near Tachi from the plane, which frightened him off long enough to allow the pilot to get the foal into the helicopter.

Then we had to get in. As we retreated, Tachi chased us and kicked out at us again. And even as we scrambled into the helicopter he kicked the machine as it took off, leaving two deep hoof marks in the metal.

But we had the foal, and when my father had a chance to look at it in the helicopter we knew we had done the right thing, because its eyes were already filmed over blue, and it could not have lasted much longer down there without its mother.

What else can I say, Kitty?

We cleaned the little foal and wrapped it in a warm skin and kept it in one of our tents. We fed it ourselves, and every day it seemed to be living, or it seemed to be dying. We never knew which.

In the meantime we had to do something about Peep and Tachi. We, who live with horses, know very well that one horse can pine away when its mate dies. We have all seen it happen many times. So we wondered what we could do about Tachi.

When we flew over the valley again we saw that Tachi was still standing over Peep. What else could he do? And what else could we do but bury her there in our far away mountains; in our dry, brown, Altai grasslands? We had to keep Tachi away with noise and whip cracks and sticks while we dug a grave for your poor little pony. There she lies now, and I hope you will forgive our wild horse for bringing her so far away from home, only to die of exhaustion and suffering in our empty valley. Such a terrible fate after all her devotion.

Even when we took off again in the helicopter, Tachi came back and looked around desperately for her. He knew where we had buried her, and he began to root at the place with his hoofs and his nose. Four days later he was still there, and we dropped him some food. On the eleventh day he had gone.

By that time we were sure that the little foal would survive. We had him up on his feet, but our real problem was to find a foster mother for him, and we decided to persuade an old and friendly mare (who had a foal of her own) to take him.

Unfortunately, our domestic horses always know when there is something wild in a foal, and we thought it would be difficult to persuade the old mare. But it was not. Peep's foal is a very docile little fellow, anxious to follow everybody around, and he just walked up to the old mare as if she was expecting him. She bit him once to tell him that she was boss, and then he simply stuck to her.

That is all there is to say, Kitty, except that a week later Gritti witnessed the final and inevitable struggle between Tachi and the young stallion. Of course Tachi won. He pummelled and bit and simply annihilated the young stallion, who fought bravely, but also wildly and stupidly according to Gritti. He eventually ran away. Thereafter Tachi bit every horse in the herd, even the foals. Gritti says he also licked them with his tongue, but my father says that is impossible. In any case Tachi is finally master of the herd that he was so anxious to return to, and he is already looking for a way out of the mountains. So now we will have a very difficult job keeping the herd confined. Eventually the young stallion came back and joined them, so they are finally one unit again.

Gritti asked the Academy of Sciences if they intended to recapture Tachi and send him back to you. There was no answer for a week. Then five scientists arrived from Ulan Bator to see our remarkable wild horse. When they heard all the details, they decided on the spot that it was pointless trying to take Tachi away from his mountains. He would always set out to return, no matter where he was taken to. So Tachi will remain with us forever.

We thought at first that we ought to keep the little foal in our domestic herd, as well, but after a meeting in which everybody took part (all my family and the scientists and Gritti and the neighbours) we all decided unanimously that we would send the foal back to you, Kitty. In this way you would have a good memory of us, as well as of your little mare Peep, who crossed all Europe and Asia to be with Tachi. She was a loyal and brave horse, which is what we Mongolians think of as the best thing in the world next to a good friend and a loyal comrade.

We do not know when the foal will be sent. Probably when it is able to travel, and when it no longer needs its foster mother.

In the meantime, Kitty, I hope that you are finding your new home in Portsmouth a happy place. So many sad things happen to all of us, that anything which is not cruel or ugly or wrong is worth a great deal, don't you think? This has been a sad letter, and I did not want to write it. But perhaps it will have a happy ending. I hope so, Kitty.

Your ever loyal friend,
Baryut

21

Dear Baryut,

I thought I would weep buckets when I realized half-way through your letter what was going to happen to Peep. I knew it! But I don't seem to weep anymore. Not at the right things, anyway. Usually it's for the wrong and silly things.

Nonetheless I wept inwardly for Peep, and every time I go to visit Grandfather and Mrs Evans (every week-end), I still feel as if Peep is walking around just behind me. I don't think I'll ever be able to look out on our hillsides without remembering our teasing games of hide and seek there.

But I'm glad that Peep stuck to Tachi through thick and thin. Grandfather says that only something that was worthwhile could have made them stick together like that. Grandfather is now resigned to the fact that he will never see

Tachi again. But Mrs Evans wept buckets when I read her your letter, and she said she was very sorry that she had sometimes shouted angrily at Peep. Grandfather had to tell her not to be foolish. That in fact she had spoiled Peep, as we all did. Which made Mrs Evans feel much better. We all wait anxiously and impatiently now to see Peep's foal.

I like my new home in Portsmouth, although I do miss the Reserve and Grandfather and Mrs Evans. I have Skip with me, which makes me feel a bit better. But everything will be all right when I get used to my father and step-mother. They are very kind and considerate, and only try to help. Though I don't even know myself half the time what the matter is. I wish I did know.

Well, that's all I can write, Baryut. But many thanks for your long letter, even though it was so sad. I send a special embrace to your mother and to your Aunt Seroghli for all her trouble and patience, and her wonderful English.

Yours ever,
Kitty

PS I've been skiing twice, and my parents are going to take me to Switzerland next winter, which will be marvellous if I don't pitch over and break a leg. I *love* skiing. K.

* * * * *

Dear Kitty,

The foal, whom we have named Katch, left here last week, and Gritti says it will arrive in England by plane on the 15th of the month, with the young master stallion whom Tachi defeated. We decided to send him to your grandfather!! Let me know when Katch arrives. I only wish I was going with him to visit you.

Yours,
Baryut

* * * * *

Dear Baryut,

The foal has arrived (but not the stallion yet), and I couldn't help laughing hysterically the moment I saw him. He is so pretty and so ugly at the same time. But even though I laughed it was the right kind of laugh. He has Peep's soft eyes, but he also has Tachi's funny beard and head and stripes and snort. I think he walks like Tachi, with that fierce little shake of a wild horse. Which is very funny, because he's so tame and so affectionate. Even more so than Peep was. Mrs Evans won't let him out of her sight. She would probably let him into the kitchen if Grandfather didn't forbid it. She dotes on him all the time, and he dotes on her, and on me too.

I think of you *very often* these days, probably because of the foal, and I wish more than ever that you lived nearer. I'd love to see you and talk to you. I long to talk to someone. Couldn't you come somehow to see me, to see the foal?

In fact, isn't it odd that our two horses were able to travel the whole world, right across the continents of Europe and Asia, through frontiers and over high mountains, defying storms and snow and mud and trouble, and yet you and I can only write to each other.

So please try to come. Tell me if I can do anything to make it possible. I really long to see you . . .

Your everlasting friend,
Kitty

PS Please try!

*   *   *   *   *

Dear Kitty,

Of course I will try to come to see you. But I think it is easier for you to come here. We would give you such a welcome. All
136

my family would be so happy. I would then feel that everything that Tachi and Peep did had been worthwhile, if only because it brought you out here to see us. I could take you everywhere over our mountains and grasslands, and then we could ride up on our hills, and nobody need bother us. Perhaps we can even look for our five missing wild horses. Do try, Kitty, and I promise to do everything to help.

Your close friend,
Baryut

$$* \quad * \quad * \quad * \quad *$$

Dear Baryut,

I can hardly believe it, but it's actually possible (just possible!) that I might be coming to see you, if I can get permission to come with Grandfather. I kept asking Grandfather and begging him, and finally he said he will try to arrange it. Perhaps I can come with him. I don't know. But I'm trying desperately. Desperately . . .

Yours ever,
Kitty

PS I am sending you a new photograph of myself in case you think I'm the same as I was before. Nothing is ever the same for long, is it, particularly me. That's the trouble, I suppose. Everything always changes so quickly, doesn't it? All the time. K.

$$* \quad * \quad * \quad * \quad *$$

Dear Kitty,

I have asked Gritti to help you to get permission to come. Gritti says he will do everything possible. He has gone to Ulan

Bator to see our professors there. He swears he will arrange everything for you.

Yours,
B.

*　　*　　*　　*　　*

Dear B.,

I still can't believe it. But it's all arranged!

Grandfather got a telegram from Ulan Bator inviting him to a 'Seminar on the Wild Horse' in the Academy of Sciences at Ulan Bator. They also invited me with him, as a special guest. So I'll actually (incredibly!) be seeing you very soon. I feel so happy about it, Baryut, that I could burst! I already feel the way Peep must have felt, setting out on a long journey with something unknown at the end of it. I wonder what it will be?

But you must make sure you are there at Ulan Bator to meet me. I couldn't bear it if you weren't. I wouldn't know what to do. So please be there to meet me. Please . . .

K.

PS Katch finally got into Mrs Evans's kitchen, and she made him lie down in the corner. She refused to let Grandfather throw him out. Please be there when I arrive!! K.

*　　*　　*　　*　　*

Dear Kitty,

I write this in English. I will be there. I think about seeing you. I do not know what to say. I say that it will be a wonderful day for me. I will be very happy! I hope it will also be the same for

you. We will be like our two wonderful and beautiful horses, Tachi and Peep. I think we will now be friends forever. I do await you impatiently, and with everything ready.

With many affections from your loyal
comrade and friend and brother,
Baryut Mingha

Piccolo fiction

Eva Ibbotson
The Great Ghost Rescue 40p

Modernization has driven the ghosts from their rightful haunts and
threatened them with extinction, but Rick decides to help them!
The Gliding Kilt (legless), the smelly Hag, Wailing Winifred and
Headless Aunt Hortensia don't really mean to make you laugh,
but they are helplessly funny.

Arthur C. Clarke
Dolphin Island 40p

This exciting story is set in the 21st century on an island in the
Great Barrier Reef. Johnny, who has run away from home and
hidden aboard an inter-continental hovership, is shipwrecked in
the middle of the South Pacific Ocean. Stranded on a raft, he is
miraculously propelled by a pack of dolphins towards the famous
centre for dolphin research.

Johnny is allowed to stay on the island and assist in training the
dolphins. He goes skin diving at night, survives a fearful hurricane
and unearths a horrifying underwater conspiracy.

Harriet Graham
A Fox Under My Jacket 25p

Paul and Jo, newly arrived from the country, hate everything about
London. Then they find a family of foxes on Hampstead Heath.
The vixen is killed on the railway line and the boys look after her
two starving cubs secretly in their garden shed. But trouble starts
when the local gang of boys gets to hear about it . . .

Ruth Park
The Hole in the Hill 40p

What was the secret of Three-Mile Farm?
What caused the bloodcurdling wails at night?
Where did the underground caverns lead?
Was the proud young Maori boy friend or foe?

Fourteen-year-old Brownie Mackenzie and her younger brother
Dunk went to the New Zealand countryside for a quiet holiday.
Instead they found themselves on the threshold of thrilling
adventures — with more than a hint of danger.

Michael Hardcastle
Goals in the Air 35p

You will enjoy reading this book about sixteen-year-old Kenny, who plays for Second Division Marton Rangers. He has a talent for goal-scoring and turns half-chances into goals. This brings praise from the crowd, but his family, team-mates and girlfriend all bring problems that he finds difficult to handle ...